Surrender

By

Kimberly Zant

Erotic Romance

New Concepts   Georgia

Be sure to check out our website for the very best in fiction at fantastic prices!

When you visit our webpage, you can:
* Read excerpts of currently available books
* View cover art of upcoming books and current releases
* Find out more about the talented artists who capture the magic of the writer's imagination on the covers
* Order books from our backlist
* Find out the latest NCP and author news--including any upcoming book signings by your favorite NCP author
* Read author bios and reviews of our books
* Get NCP submission guidelines
* And so much more!

We offer a 20% discount on all new Trade Paperback releases ordered from our website!

Be sure to visit our webpage to find the best deals in e-books and paperbacks! To find out about our new releases as soon as they are available, please be sure to sign up for our newsletter
(http://www.newconceptspublishing.com/newsletter.htm) or join our reader group
(http://groups.yahoo.com/group/new_concepts_pub/join)!

The newsletter is available by double opt in only and our customer information is *never* shared!

Visit our webpage at:
www.newconceptspublishing.com

New Concepts Publishing, Inc.
5202 Humphreys Rd.
Lake Park, GA 31636

ISBN 978-1-58608-899-6
© February 2007 Kimberly Zant
Cover art (c) copyright February 2007 Jenny Dixon

NCP books are available at special quantity discounts for bulk purchases for sales promotions, premiums, fund raising, or educational use. For details, write, email, or phone New Concepts Publishing, Inc., 5202 Humphreys Rd., Lake Park, GA 31636; Ph. 229-257-0367, Fax 229-219-1097; orders@newconceptspublishing.com.

First NCP Trade Paperback Printing: March 2007

Chapter One

I suppose I should have found the wording of the contract reassuring, because it certainly indicated that everything was completely above board and the dark fears circling the back of my mind like a flock of black crows were groundless. Instead, a sense of unreality swept through me as I read back over the long list of terms I was agreeing to, tying my nervous stomach into a harder knot.

Desperation, I thought, looking up at the man seated across from me, was a hard task master—and destitution the equivalent of hell on earth because the fear of it was enough to make an ordinarily rational person, like myself, consider making a deal with the devil.

He didn't look like the devil. He looked like a completely ordinary mortal.

"Is there a problem?"

I cleared my throat, which felt as if it had closed together. "It says if I fail to ... uh ... fail to perform according to expectations, I can be terminated immediately without compensation."

He gave me an impatient look. "I explained that to you when you applied for the position. Would you like to go over everything again?"

He had. I'd just been too addled to really take it in, because from the moment I'd realized exactly what I was being hired to do my mind had gone perfectly blank.

I felt my face redden. "It's just ... does that mean if he isn't satisfied with my performance? Or, by fail, does it mean if I refused to do anything I'd agreed to do? I did mention that I hadn't actually done much of this before? A lot of these things, I mean. The things on the list aren't ... aren't really familiar to me, experience wise, so I couldn't really claim to be good at this."

He looked a little uncomfortable. "That clause goes to willingness to perform the various ... acts that have been described. A refusal to do so upon demand would be a breach of contract, which would make all terms null and void. The client is aware of your relative inexperience."

I nodded at the clarification, though I didn't feel terribly reassured. I felt like kicking myself. The money being offered was staggering considering it was only for a six week stint. I wasn't stupid. I had known going in to the first interview that it had to be something really radical for them to be offering so much. Lying to myself wasn't going to change a thing. I'd suspected, just from the wording of the ad, in spite of how carefully it had been composed, that this was, in effect, sex for hire. As shocked and horrified as I'd been once everything had been baldly laid out for me, though, I hadn't gotten up and walked out. I'd stayed and listened to the entire spiel, and I'd allowed them to interview me. The list of 'requirements' was part of the initial interview.

They'd been very cool and professionally impersonal about it, but I'd cringed inside and stumbled over every answer.

I suppose I'd never really believed that they would actually offer the position to me. I was hardly sex goddess material, and I was certain my prudishness must be glaringly obvious, which would also make it evident that my knowledge and experience of the subject under discussion was practically nil.

I'd known before I'd even arrived for the interview, though, that I couldn't afford to turn it down, whatever it entailed—short of murder. I needed the money way too badly to worry about silly old things like pride or morals or even doing things I might not especially like. People who weren't facing disaster and starvation could afford to have principles. I couldn't.

'Whatever sexual acts requested' though—why, I wondered, would they have any interest in me? I'd seen the competition. Most of the other women had been younger than me—college age young, pretty, well built. A lot of them had had that 'road weary' look that proclaimed a vast deal of sexual experience, and I'd been sure one of them would be chosen. Why would they choose a 'ripe' tomato like me, who was not the least bit girlish in any way? I'd had two children, and I had the 'womanly' body to prove it. Sure I'd tried really hard to battle nature, because my husband--ex husband--had brow beat me about 'letting myself go' until I was terrified gaining five pounds would earn me the boot, but no amount of dieting or exercise could undo what carrying a baby for nine months could do to a body, let alone going through it twice.

Maybe it was the 'submissive' thing?

I was certainly *used* to being submissive, and I supposed that showed. I hadn't been terribly assertive before my marriage and, having been a total idiot and bound myself to a tyrant with serious control issues, the little assertiveness I'd had before had been crushed under his heavy hand.

Regardless, I still wasn't certain I could carry this off.

My ex was going to get my children, though, if I didn't come up with a *lot* of money fast, I reminded myself.

For *them*, I could be a tigress. I *would* be—a submissive one, granted, but the *will* to take this on, that was mine.

Smiling weakly, I took up the pen.

"If you decide to terminate the agreement at any time, you have that option, but the full payment will not be due to you. It will be prorated according to time put in."

I looked at him blankly.

"For instance, half if you only stay three weeks instead of the full six."

I nodded, dragging in a shaky breath. I could do this. I needed *all* the money.

When I'd signed it, he notarized the contract and got up to run off a copy for me. He handed me a card with an address on it after he'd handed me a copy. "You're to report to this address tomorrow morning."

I stared at the card, feeling faint that everything seemed to be moving so fast. "He didn't want to meet me first?"

"*They*," he corrected. "It was a group that selected this fantasy holiday. They were present at the interview, observing from the room adjoining, and selected you from among the other applicants."

"Group?" I asked weakly, feeling more faint. I wasn't certain what startled me more, the discovery that they'd been watching me while I was interviewed or the 'group' part. Actually, I was certain. It hadn't occurred to me, at all, that it would be a group. And that unnerved me a lot more than the fact that I'd been watched without my knowledge.

He gave me an irritated look. "Is that a problem?"

I swallowed with an effort. Safety was assured. I'd had a thorough health exam before I was even allowed to interview and the same was required of 'guests'. No one, least of all the company, wanted to have to face the unpleasant repercussions of a lawsuit. Moreover, I would be allowed to call it off at any point and a company representative would be checking in every other day to make certain none of the rules had been violated. It *had* to be voluntary. That was part of his—their—fantasy. "No," I said weakly, realizing that it had probably taken a group to fork out the money the company was asking for this arrangement plus the money I was getting.

"The money has already been deposited in a holding account. You'll be given the access number once you've completed the job. And, of course, if you decide to terminate early, the amount unearned will be removed from the account before you're given the number."

Dismissed, I had nothing to do but leave, but it took a supreme effort to push myself up from the chair. Wobbly kneed, completely addled by the thoughts rattling my brain, I stuffed the card and my copy of the contract into my purse and let myself out.

I sat staring into space for a while once I'd gotten into my car.

I'd just signed away six weeks of my life to play submissive sex toy to a 'group' of men I'd never even set eyes on.

Think positive, I told myself. Six weeks wasn't a lot when it meant at the end of it my troubles with my ex would be over.

I can do this, I told myself.

My mother was never going to know. All she knew at this point was that she was babysitting for six weeks so I could take a job that would guarantee I had the money to win my case and get custody of my children.

If I didn't freak and do anything stupid, *nobody* was ever going to know.

* * * *

I ran out of steam before I got to the door of the mansion. Breathless with fear and weak all over, it took all I could do to manage the last few steps and ring the doorbell … and to fight the urge to whirl around and flee, though, in all honesty, I wasn't sure I had the strength to flee.

Partly, it was the mansion itself that intimidated me. I was certain, at first, that I must have the address wrong, but after studying the card and the house number for ten minutes, I decided I wasn't hallucinating. The mansion, I decided, must belong to the company, the 'game group' that arranged these entertaining little fantasies for the truly wealthy and jaded, or in my case, the well-to-do and jaded and/or kinky. I wasn't certain where that put my little group, but I had already decided that it was a group because they couldn't afford an individual 'game', which still put them in a staggering income bracket if they could afford to pay me thousands *and* take off for a six week 'vacation'.

Facing the unknown was rather akin to facing a firing squad, though, and that was the biggest part of my anxiety. True, I had a dim idea of what I was facing, but it was just enough to scare me shitless.

The man that answered the doorbell didn't look like a butler, despite my expectations to the contrary. In point of fact, and despite my anxieties, the moment we made eye contact a stunning force of attraction rolled over me that demolished the last of my wits.

He was tall and dark—thirtyish I thought, maybe late twenties. His face was unquestionably attractive in a very manly-male way, though not precisely handsome, his build, at least from what I could tell considering the expensive suit he was wearing, was just as appealing as the face.

He looked me up and down with a slow thoroughness that made me feel naked which should have insulted me, or intimidated me even more, but instead had the effect of making my heart rev and warmth flutter in my belly. "Anna," he said finally. "Prompt. I like that."

He didn't sound like a butler either. His voice was deep and fired synapses in my brain as if he'd reached out and run a caressing hand over my breasts.

He didn't look at me like a servant … or at least the way I thought a servant would look at a guest.

"Come in," he said after a moment. "I'll show you to your room and then we can get down to business."

I blinked, undecided now whether he *was* in fact the butler, or one of the 'group' I was to meet. Nodding jerkily, I followed him across the expansive marble tiled foyer and up a wide, winding stairway to the second floor. Carpet, so thick I felt as if I was wading through water, covered the upper hallway. He led me down it to a bedroom on the back side of the house and opened the door, indicating that I was to go in.

My heart was in my throat as I preceded him and set my small bag on the floor by the huge four poster bed that held center stage in the room. I got a fleeting impression of opulence everywhere, in the massive, ornately carved furniture, the heavy drapes, thick carpet and expensive knickknacks here and there, but I was too nervous to gawk. As soon as I'd set my battered little suitcase down, I turned to face him uneasily.

He closed the door. Folding his arms, he leaned back against the panel, studying me. It made me uneasy that I couldn't tell anything about his expression.

"You were acquainted with the rules and the list of what we expect of you?"

The question was unexpected. I blinked at him and finally nodded speechlessly, unable even to find my voice for a polite 'yes'.

His dark brows inched up his forehead. "Just the same, I think I'll go over them," he said. Pushing away from the door, he approached me, and I realized abruptly that he was a good bit taller and broader than I'd first thought.

"You are a submissive and as such will be expected to obey without question anything I, or the others, ask of you. We are familiar with the list. We compiled it, and nothing will be asked of you that you have not willingly agreed to, in writing. Therefore no, is no longer a part of your vocabulary. You have been given a safety word, but I will not expect to hear it unless you are ready to throw in the towel."

My mouth felt like the Mohave desert. I swallowed with an effort and managed to nod again that I understood.

"Take off your clothes and let me have a look at you."

I felt my eyes widen, but as his dark brows descended, I looked down and began to fumble nervously with the buttons of my blouse. He watched me keenly while I stripped, unnerving me more. By the time I'd stripped down to my bra and panties my face was flashing like a neon sign and the red went all the way down to my breasts. I looked up at him a little hopefully when I'd gotten to that point—hopeful that was as far as I would be expected to go.

No such luck.

"The rest," he said implacably.

Dragging in a shuddering breath, I complied, resisting the urge to try to cover myself with my hands and completely unable to figure out what to do with them when it dawned on me that I shouldn't try to cover myself. I flinched in spite of all I could do when he reached for my breasts but gritted my teeth and held perfectly still while he examined them, letting out a shaky breath when he released them after a moment and walked around me, looking me over with a slow attention to detail that I felt sure missed no flaw.

His eyes were dark and smoldering with heat when he faced me again. Reaching down, he dragged his fingers through the curls at the apex of my thighs, making me jump. "Au natural," he said speculatively. "Appealing, and yet I like to be able to see my pretty thing."

I felt my face heat again as he withdrew his gaze from my mound and met mine. As if that settled something in his mind, he moved away, striding toward a door I hadn't noticed before. Opening it, he turned to look at me expectantly. "Come along, Anna. First a bath and then I'll trim that."

Trim that? My hair *there*?

Submissive! I reminded myself and moved toward him jerkily, standing dumbstruck while he adjusted the water in the huge tub that looked as if it could easily accommodate a half a dozen people at one time—three or four anyway.

Indicating with a nod that I was to get in, I did so, settling almost with a sense of relief because me legs had felt as if they would give way and dump me in the floor at any moment.

Taking up a position near the door, he watched me bathe. I wasn't sure if that was because he wanted to make certain I was thorough, or if he merely wanted to watch, but I reminded myself, again, that I had, to all intents and purposes, contracted to be his sex slave for the duration and that meant he did whatever he pleased and I submitted to whatever he pleased—as long as it didn't violate the rules I'd agreed to.

And it occurred to me rather forcefully as I mentally reviewed those rules that I'd agreed to pretty much anything so long as it didn't entail injury to me.

Either the hot water or just plain old weariness began to dissipate the tension as I bathed, slowly, not because I was trying to give him a show but because I felt awkward at being watched. I wasn't even *almost* relaxed, but the edge wore off.

It felt strange to be watched, made me conscious of every moment of my hands in a way I never had been before. On the other hand, despite my nervousness, there was no doubt in my mind that his gaze was appreciative, and it warmed me in a purely sensual way.

I would've been willing to sit in the tub until my skin pruned since being watched wasn't nearly as unnerving as some of the thoughts rambling through my chaotic brain, but he moved away from the door after a few minutes and picked up a thick towel. Instead of handing it to me, he settled it on the top step of the two that led up to the tub and indicated that I was to get out of the tub and sit on it. My belly instantly knotted up, but I complied, sitting on the towel uneasily and placing my feet on the step below me.

Crouching in front of me, he grasped first one ankle and then the other, moving them wide apart, and then pushing my thighs wide when I kept my knees together. The instinct to snap them back together the moment he let go was strong, but one look at his face was enough to convince me not to try.

He combed his fingers through the hair on my mound and then placed his thumbs on my nether lips, pushing them apart and studying me. My color fluctuated two or three times during the process. My belly clenched and unclenched frantically, but warmth flooded my sex in spite of that, and I wondered uncomfortably if he would be able to see he made me wet just looking at me.

After studying my pussy for a handful of seconds, he grasped my hips and slid me forward until my buttocks were resting on the edge of the step and I had to put my arms behind me to keep my balance. I watched him as he got up and collected a razor and shaving cream. When he returned, kneeling between my thighs, he grasped my knees and spread my legs as wide as they would go.

The shaving cream was cold, but it was the stroke of his fingers as he applied it that made me jump, that sent shockwaves of anticipation through me and stole my breath. He flicked a glance at me as he smoothed the shaving cream between my thighs, all the way back to my rectum.

I hadn't even realized I had any hair back there. It embarrassed me to learn that I did. I tried to focus my gaze elsewhere as he began to shave me, but I couldn't help it. My gaze kept wandering back to his face.

His expression was one of concentration. It accentuated the almost harsh plains and angles of his face. His hair, somewhat longer than was currently fashionable, was very dark but not ethnic black. Rather, it was a deep, almost black, brown with just a hint of russet highlights. His brows were thick and virtually straight. His eyes would have made any woman envious. His lashes were thick, black, long, and curling, shielding eyes that were somewhere between gray and green, a pale combination of the two colors.

His nose was exceptional, too, a hawkish sort of blade but far more appealing for the sharp definition of bridge and nostrils than a fleshy blob, even though the cut of his nostrils was perilously close to a perpetual sneer. I thought it made him look extraordinarily aristocratic.

Next to his eyes, his mouth was his best feature. Wide, but not overly so, his lips were as well defined as his nose, neither too thin nor too full, and looked firm and hard like the rest of him. My belly fluttered as I stared at that mouth, and images flooded my mind of what it would feel like.

He was clean shaven, but dark hair shadowed his lean cheeks, strong jaw, and forceful chin. High testosterone, I mused, realizing that was probably a good part of my nervousness. I'd read somewhere that it actually oozed from their pores and women, even though they weren't aware they could smell it, in fact could, and it effected their libido.

As he shaved me, his brows slowly inched together in a frown of concentration and a thick lock of hair fell across his brow. He used the fingers of his free hand to stretch the fleshy outer lips of my sex taut while he shaved. It seemed impersonal, and yet I noticed after a few moments that his hand wasn't quite as steady as it had been when he'd begun.

When he flicked a glance at my face again, the green irises had virtually disappeared for the darkness of his dilated pupils.

Rising, he rinsed the razor and returned, stroking his fingers along the area he'd shaved to test his thoroughness. Apparently satisfied, he studied the wedge of hair on my belly above my cleft and trimmed it down to a small wedge that made me wonder why he'd left anything at all. I'd been denuded of hair from the beginning of my cleft all the way back and the hair on my mound trimmed until it hid nothing at all.

Leaning back slightly, he studied the effect and finally nodded. "Rinse and dry off."

He left the room while I was drying.

Wondering if we were done for now, or if he was waiting in the bedroom for my first sexual performance, I followed him uneasily after several moments and discovered that he was selecting—*something* from the armoire. My suitcase had disappeared. I felt my stomach take a freefall as I studied the garments I was, apparently, expected to wear.

Dropping them onto the bed, he summoned me to stand before a full length mirror. "This is the way I expect you to groom yourself for the duration," he said in a deep voice that sounded more than a little husky as he stood behind me and stroked a hand over my denuded pussy.

A jolt went through me at his first touch for I discovered the skin that had been covered with my pubic hair was far more sensitive than I'd ever noticed before—as if it wasn't shocking enough to *see* so clearly what had been veiled by hair before!

As I'd suspected, the little 'moustache' he left didn't cover anything. It was almost more like an exclamation point to draw attention to my pussy than anything else. The outer lips that hid my sex looked plumper than I'd thought they were and actually pretty obscene to me, but I was still relieved because my nether lips felt swollen and pouty from his focus on them, and I was glad that *that* part wasn't visible.

"The correct response is 'yes, sir'."

I struggled to find my voice and dutifully repeated the words.

"Wait here."

I watched his reflection in the mirror as he moved briskly toward the garments he'd selected. He picked up a bustier and returned. When he'd fitted the black leather piece around my waist and told me to hold it while he fastened the back, I saw that the piece only covered me from just beneath the breasts to a little more than mid-way down my hips, stopping just above my new exclamation point patch of hair. When he'd fastened it, he moved around in front of me and adjusted my breasts which were half in and half out of the thing. Scooping them from the restricting garment, he almost seemed to be 'fluffing' them. After staring at them a moment, he caught a nipple between the thumb and forefinger of each hand and plucked at them until my nipples were standing at attention and the rest of me was quivering weakly.

I saw when he moved away at last that the top of the bustier formed more of a shelf for a display than a cup, lifting my breasts as if in offering but covering nothing.

He stood behind me for several moments, studying my reflection and finally summoned me to follow him back to the bed.

He caught my chin in one hand when we stopped there, tipping my face up so that I had to meet him eye to eye. "Have you ever engaged in anal sex?"

My eyes widened. I'd been asked that as part of the interview, but I'd, conveniently, closed my mind to that. I shook my head.

He studied my face for several moments, as if he could read my mind, and finally nodded as if it was the answer he'd expected. "Turn around and lean over the bed."

I gulped, my stomach clenching harder, but oddly enough I discovered my sex was damper than before, when, by rights, the comment and all it entailed should have been enough to dry up all my juices with anxiety. Dragging in a shaky breath, I turned and did as I was told, spreading my legs wide for him and turning my head to watch as he moved to the small cabinet beside the bed, taking something from a drawer.

I'd never seen anything like the thing he pulled out. It looked strikingly similar to a dildo except that it was tapered to a narrow tip at one end and it looked as if it was made of a far softer material than dildos generally were. He squeezed lubricant out of a tube and spread it over the thing thickly. I caught my breath as he moved behind me again and pushed the cheeks of my ass wide with the fingers of one hand.

"Relax. As I insert this, you need to bear down with your stomach muscles to open the rectum."

My heart was in my throat, but as I felt him begin to push, I did as I'd been told, panting as I felt the thing penetrating me. Discomfort went through me as it penetrated, a sense of fullness followed as he pushed it slowly inside until it could go no further, but, thankfully, it wasn't nearly as uncomfortable as I'd expected.

"Now clench and hold for me and stand upright."

Disconcerted that he obviously meant to leave it, more embarrassed than uncomfortable, I pushed myself up from the bed as he returned to the nightstand. The sense of fullness increased as I straightened. It wasn't comfortable by any stretch of the imagination, but I was relieved that it wasn't painful.

I was still focused on that strange sensation of having something up my ass when he moved up behind me again. I felt a tug along the back edge of the bustier, as if he was attaching something. Catching my shoulders, he turned me to face him and knelt down. I merely stared at him when he pushed one hand between my legs. He looked up at me, his dark brows rising and nudged at my legs with his hand until I shifted them apart. Reaching between my thighs, he caught hold of whatever it was he'd attached to the back of the bustier and pulled it between my legs—into the cleft of my ass. I frowned, thinking it was just something that would be adjusted. I discovered otherwise.

It tightened as he pulled on it, pressing against my rectum and pushing the thing he'd inserted deeper. Trying not to wiggle, I stared down at the top of his dark head and his hands, unable to see what he was doing. I felt the thing cinched upward, though, felt it compress one side of the outer lips of my sex. He drew it up and fastened it to the front of the bustier, cinching it uncomfortably tight. I reached down instinctively to adjust myself, but he slapped my hand—not hard, but in rebuke.

I snatched my hand back, feeling mildly embarrassed and rather like a child that had been chastised. He delved between my legs again and pulled up another strap catching the other lip my sex as he had the first and making it obvious that it had been no accident. As he fastened the strap to the other edge of the front, cinching it as he had the first, I felt his hot breath waft over the very delicate and sensitive inner lips of my sex. My clit swelled instantly to a hard, throbbing knot and felt about twice its normal size.

He flicked a glance up at my face when he'd finished fastening the 'binding' then returned his attention to his handiwork, making minor adjustments with his fingers that made my knees feel like jelly.

"You will keep the plug in at all times unless it is necessary to remove it for your needs, then you will replace it and reattach the restraints between your legs just as I've adjusted them. In a few days, once you've grown accustomed to this one, we'll move up to a slightly larger size plug."

I stared down at his dark head, abruptly feeling mulish. I didn't want anything bigger in my ass! I already felt uncomfortable, and it boggled my mind to think I was supposed to walk around, sit, stand, whatever—trying to carry on as if I *didn't* have something shoved up my ass that was impossible to ignore or get used to.

Although the first moments of sheer terror had long since worn off, though, it had left me vulnerable to my desperate needs, allowed me the calm to realize that however reluctant I might feel, I had better keep it to myself. I hadn't expected this, but I realized I probably should have—would have if I'd had any clue about this business.

It didn't hurt. I couldn't complain to the referee, not honestly, that it did, and I knew my acceptance, and my money, depended on complete submission, which meant compliance to anything they wanted of me.

No, as he'd said, was no longer a part of my vocabulary. If I uttered my safety word, we were done and I went home as bad off as before.

He told me to sit down on the bed. When I did so, he lifted one of my legs and slipped a sheer hose over it, adjusting the elasticized upper edge on my thigh. Bending that knee, he settled my foot on the bed and lifted the other leg, repeating the process.

He sent me to stand before the mirror and study what he'd done so that I'd know how I was expected to dress hereafter.

Despite my suspicions about his adjustments, I was horrified to discover that the 'restraints' which I'd thought were primarily there to make sure the plug stayed put, pulled the outer lips of my sex back so that the darker pink inner petals were fully, obscenely exposed. It had felt 'airish'. I'd felt the brush of my thighs against sensitive flesh with every step I took, but I'd still thought I couldn't possibly *be* as exposed as I'd felt like I was.

He came to stand behind me again, this time slipping my arms into a filmy robe that was the next thing to completely transparent. He tapped my chin to make me look up at him as he tied the thin ribbon at the neck of the thing. "One final thing—You aren't allowed to cum unless you're given permission. At any time that you feel that you are about to cum, you must announce it and request permission. If, and only if, it is granted, you may cum. Otherwise, you'll be punished for disobedience. And if you make a habit of disobeying, you've failed to live up to your part of the agreement, which means it will be terminated at my discretion."

My heart tried to beat its way out of my chest at that. I stared at him owl eyed, wondering what sort of punishment they had in mind.

Nothing to do with pain or that could cause injury! That was absolutely forbidden.

I hoped he realized that.

Not that I thought I had anything to worry about. According to my ex, I was frigid. I didn't agree with him, but I had certainly never been oversexed, and I couldn't imagine having a problem containing myself.

It wasn't until a good bit later that I realized that there were ways to be punished that didn't fall under either category that were nevertheless excruciating. And not being allowed to cum, no matter what they did, was the worst of all—until I discovered the other!

Chapter Two

A pair of heels finished the ensemble. He knelt before me to slip them onto my feet. When he'd adjusted both shoes, he simply stayed where he was, looking up at me for several moments ... or rather the exposed pink lips of my sex. After a brief hesitation, he caught my legs, urging me to part them.

I stared down at his dark head as I did so, wondering what he meant to do.

A shock wave rolled over me when he opened his mouth over my clit. My knees instantly turned to water as he tugged at it with his mouth, sucked it, and then tugged again. Heat rolled through my mind, making me feel weak all over and making it almost impossible to maintain my balance. Mindlessly, I dug my fingers into his hair as he continued licking and sucking until I was shaking all over and thought I'd wilt to the floor.

He disentangled my fingers, caught my wrists and held them at my sides.

A soft moan escaped me in spite of all I could do to contain it. Almost as if he'd been waiting for that reaction, he stopped. Rising to his feet he studied my face for several moments and finally told me to follow him.

I stared after him blankly for several moments and finally, as he reached the door, managed to command my feet to move. I was in a daze, however, as I followed him down the stairs, and it took every ounce of concentration to keep my wobbly legs from buckling.

I was so dazed still as I followed him down the lower hallway and into a room that it was several moments before I realized there were men in the room awaiting us.

"There," the man leading me said, pointing to a spot on the floor.

I stopped, wondering if I was supposed to sit down or just stand.

The other men rose and approached me.

There were four—five if I counted the first.

Surprise was my first impression, because I was still too rattled by what he had done and my racing pulse to feel much of anything else. Not one of them looked to be more than their late twenties and the plainest of the group was what I would've considered 'nice' looking any day of the week.

I had been trying very hard since I discovered the day before that I was to entertain a group *not* to consider what sort of men would pay so much for a submissive, but it had nagged at the back of my mind that they would *not* be the sort of men who could get a woman without paying for her.

These men were as far from hideous, wrinkled old men as they could possibly get. I was fairly certain that not one was even as old as I was. They were clean cut, well dressed—expensively dressed, handsome, well built.

Why in the world, I wondered, would they even consider hiring a woman, much less me?

But then maybe the buzz from that tongue lashing I had gotten on my clit had really scrambled my brains?

I studied them uneasily as they studied me, flinching in spite of all I could do as first one and then another lifted a hand and caressed a breast, an arm, a thigh, my buttocks. One of the men bore a striking resemblance to the man who had been grooming me, and I knew he had to be related. He was a little taller, I thought, and had a slighter build, though he was a long way from skinny. Two of them were blonds, although one of the two had more of a strawberry blond hair color and the other an ash blond. The fifth had blue black hair and was swarthy enough I thought he might have had a drop or two of some ethnic mix—but it eluded me what that might have been. Of them all, he was the most exotically, classically handsome, borderline 'pretty boy' but just a hair too manly looking with his square jaw and five o'clock shadow to earn that sobriquet.

Their personalities, I fancied, were reflected on their faces as they looked me over. The one with ash blond hair was either shy or just reserved. His expression was guarded. He didn't touch, but he looked me over thoroughly. I saw a deep hunger in his gaze as he lifted his head to study my face that made everything inside of me grow hot and jittery.

'Pretty boy' had the look of a player. He was struggling to maintain an air of bored interest, but I could see that his eyes were stormy and his hand shook faintly as he stroked it over my breast and watched my nipple pucker and stand erect. I sensed a good deal of tension in him, as if he was controlling himself with an effort, but that made it all the more obvious that what he really wanted to do at that very moment was to throw me down on the couch or floor and fuck me senseless.

The man with the strawberry blond hair was open faced and, I thought, probably impetuous. He looked more like a randy teenager who could hardly contain his glee than a man approaching thirty.

The one I had decided must be related to my groomer also had the 'air' of a player.

My groomer, who had taken up a position by the fireplace while the others looked me over, seemed by far the most dark and dangerous of the bunch and the hardest to read. I had the impression that he was eldest, certainly the ringmaster, but it was more a matter of his aplomb than that he actually appeared older.

They moved away after a few moments, settling in their seats again.

I was told to sit by the man who had prepared me. Moving to the couch he had indicated, I sat—very carefully. Sitting, I discovered, nearly coming up off the couch again the second my ass hit it, pressed the plug I had almost been able to dismiss from my mind more deeply inside of me and the restraints pulled uncomfortably at the lips of my sex. He shook his head. "Not like that. We like being able to see you."

He moved toward me. Directing me to put my arms behind me to brace myself and lean back, he grasped my knees and parted my thighs and then stepped back to study the effect. "When you're allowed to sit in our presence, you will sit like that to display our pretty pussy for us."

I felt my face reddening as he moved away again, and I saw that the others were studying me. A warm wetness filled my channel, however, as I felt their gazes on me—or rather their 'pretty pussy'. It was more than a little unnerving to draw that many avid gazes, because none of them made any great attempt at that point even to pretend they weren't interested in what I was displaying for them. I saw Adam's apples bobbing. It made my own mouth go dry, and the fear assailed me that, displayed as I was, they were going to see the effect their interest had on me.

I had gone beyond damp. I felt downright wet, and I feared they already could see the effect, and that was one of the reasons I could see a definite response against their breeches.

"Yes. I like that," said one of the men, clearing his throat before he spoke, the strawberry blond who looked to be around twenty five but might have been older.

"Anna, this is Chance," my groomer said, indicating the man that had spoken. "I'm Kaelen. The tall guy with the black hair is Dev, the blond, Cameron, and the skinny one there is my brother, Gareth. You may refer to us as by our given name, or sir."

I was actually surprised he hadn't ordered me to refer to them as lord or master. I blinked a few times as I assimilated that and finally merely nodded, wondering if I would remember a single name if it actually became necessary to use it.

Submissive, I reminded myself—whatever he had said, they were all my lords and masters for the duration and whatever doubts I had had before that they would take full advantage and enjoy it thoroughly vanished. There was no reluctance and no conflict on any other their faces. Rather, they seemed to be struggling to hold back the urge to instantly sample their submissive.

I could do this, I thought, fighting a battle of my own.

The plug was an uncomfortable reminder that they were going to expect things of me that I wasn't used to doing, had never done, but they weren't at all hard on the eyes. That, I felt sure, would make it easier.

I hoped.

To my surprise, once he had made the introductions, the other men got to their feet and left. Kaelen settled in a chair across from me, studying me through slumberous eyes for several moments before he lifted a hand and crooked a finger at me. I got up with an effort and crossed to him. "Down on your knees."

My sex clenched spasmodically and so did my rectum around the plug, or maybe it was the second that caused the first? I got down on my knees, waiting for further instruction, watching with a mixture of uneasiness and, surprisingly, to me at least, almost a sense of breathless anticipation as he unfastened his belt and then pulled his zipper down. "Pleasure me."

My mouth went dry, but not from reluctance. After staring at him for several moments, waiting for him to produce the cock I had been told to suck, I realized he was waiting for me to get it out myself. My hands shook as I delved the folds of his trousers and found the opening in his shorts. His cock was already hard and throbbing when I pulled it free of his clothing.

It was huge, to my eyes at least, but then again I wasn't used to looking at one quite this closely in broad daylight. It was long and thick, though. I discovered as I curled my hand around the hard shaft that my hand didn't span the circumference. His skin was smooth and surprisingly silky to the touch. The veins that ran the length were prominent. The rounded head was glossy. A tiny drop of moisture beaded the slit in the end.

I stared at that drop of moisture feeling my belly go weightless. My salivary glands went into over time, burning as they spasmed.

I flicked a glance at his face and finally shifted closer, opening my mouth and engulfing the glossy head. Surprise and pleasure flooded me as the taste and texture of his cock filled my mouth. Without conscious intent, I licked the slit at the tip, collecting the drop of moisture that had mesmerized me. A dizzying wave of heat rushed over me, and I sucked the head with far more enthusiasm, using my tongue to explore the shape of it and trace the ridge just beneath his cock head.

He shifted a little restlessly. I wasn't certain if it was because he was impatient for me to take the whole thing into my mouth or because he liked what I was doing, but I opened my mouth wider and allowed his cock to slide as deeply into my mouth as I could, sucking on it as I lifted my head again. I released it, looking up at him. "Like that?"

I knew the mechanics of giving head, of course, but I had never gotten the impression that I was particularly good at it.

His voice was harsh when he spoke and gravelly, as if with disuse. "Just like that. I want to cum in your mouth. I want you to suck me dry. You'd like that, wouldn't you, Anna?"

His voice, his words were strangely seductive, evoking a response inside of me I hardly recognized at first. My gaze flickered over his lean, handsome face, lingered for a long moment on his mouth and finally settled on his eyes. "Yes," I answered finally, realizing that I did, recognizing finally that the unidentifiable sensation I had felt was a hunger that demanded appeasement.

"Yes, what?" he demanded, his voice a little hoarser than before.

"Yes … Kaelen," I responded, my own voice husky with arousal.

Something flickered in his eyes. I had a sense that it was part surprise and, strangely enough, that my response had worked on him much the same as his had worked on me, aroused him even more. He settled his hand over mine where I gripped his cock. His hand dwarfed mine, covered it completely. Slowly, he guided my hand over his cock, teaching me the way he wanted to be pleasured.

"My dick is sensitive all over, root to tip, and all the way around," he murmured huskily as he guided my hand in a massage that brought pressure to bear all the way around and from root to tip. My balls, too." His eyes slid almost shut as he guided my hand to his testicles, and I massaged them carefully, a little unnerved because I knew how easily a man could be hurt there.

The weight of his hand on mine stirred currents inside of me as surely as the feel of his cock beneath my hand did. I was almost disappointed when he lifted his hand at last.

Dragging in a shaky breath, I continued to massage him as he had shown me, pausing now and then to suck the head of his cock and tease it with my tongue, sometimes taking as much of his cock into my mouth as I could and sucking his flesh. He remained perfectly still at first, but then, almost as if he could no longer bear to remain still, he began to move with me, thrusting upward as I stroked downward on his cock, surging into my mouth when I closed my mouth around him. My excitement seemed to grow apace with his, and I began to stroke him faster as he moved more and more restlessly, his breath hitching in his chest and then sawing outward in harsh bursts of breath that grew more and more ragged. The hunger in me grew until I was suckling his flesh greedily, more focused on that than massaging him with my hand.

Uttering a sound that was part growl, part groan, he speared his fingers through my hair, clenching them tightly against my skull as his cock bucked in my mouth. My heart clenched. Drawing him deeply inside my mouth, I sucked harder. The hot, salty taste of his semen filled my mouth. I groaned, swallowing and lapping at him hungrily, sucking on his cock as if I could suck his seed from him. A shudder went through him as his body convulsed in orgasm. His harsh breaths became almost pained grunts as I milked him until he had no more to yield and continued to suck at him hungrily until he finally pushed me away.

He was gasping for breath when I lifted my head, his head tipped back against the chair. As if he felt my gaze, he lifted his head after a moment. His eyes were blazing as he stared down at me. His hands tightened around my skull, tugging me upward as he leaned forward, his gaze fastened with intent upon my mouth.

For several painful heartbeats I was certain he meant to kiss me. He hesitated within inches of my lips, though, his gaze flicking to mine. Something flickered in his eyes, caution, doubt, a sudden realization. I had no clear idea if I was right on any point. Slowly, he released his grip on my head and leaned back. I saw his throat move as he swallowed.

"Good girl," he said finally, his voice still hoarse.

It took me several moments to realize that it was a dismissal.

Disappointment flooded me as he looked away from me, focusing his attention on adjusting himself, and then zipped his pants. Anger flickered to life behind the disappointment, because my body was screaming for release—as certain as I had been before that that was not going to be an issue for me. He had made a point of telling me, in point of fact, that I wasn't allowed to cum without permission.

With an effort I tamped it as it dawned on me that I had been hired—hired to submit to them, not to receive pleasure. I was a toy, not a person, and my feelings were of no consequence—in fact shouldn't even be an issue, I realized.

He wasn't my lover. He was my employer.

I felt like kicking myself, then.

He wasn't in the wrong. I was. I had let myself get carried away and 'forgotten' that this wasn't something I was doing because I wanted to. It was a job I had taken because I desperately needed money.

Uncertain of what I was supposed to do now, I returned to my seat on the sofa. He glanced at me frowningly as he got to his feet. It took me a second to realize what that frown was for.

Leaning back, I spread my legs, trying to ignore the fact that my clit was swollen with my own needs now and throbbing hard enough to make me miserable.

His brow cleared. He moved toward me, stood over me for several moments and finally leaned down. Currents of heat went through me and directly to my core as he sucked one of my nipples into his mouth, bit down on it just hard enough to make me suck in my breath, and then lathed it with his tongue.

And then abandoned me.

Despite the pep talk I had just had with myself, I sat fuming when he had gone. Contrary to all that was logical, having my nether lips exposed to the cool air did *not* cool me down. As time passed, I began to realize that it was the very fact that I was so exposed that my engines refused to cool.

Left alone, I began to wonder if the rule of 'sitting' still applied when no one was around. Before I had entirely decided whether I could get comfortable or not, the door opened.

Much to my disappointment, I saw it wasn't Kaelen.

Gareth looked like a leaner, slightly scaled down version of his brother, at least physically, though I thought he might be a fraction taller. His hair, although still closer to black than brown, was a lighter shade than Kaelen's, his face slightly less angular. Studied objectively, I supposed his features were actually closer to handsome than his brother's, too, and yet, to me, Kaelen seemed to exude a more powerful magnetism.

He took the seat Kaelen had sat in earlier, crooking a finger at me in a gesture strikingly familiar. I got up and crossed to stand in front of him.

"On your knees, here," he said, indicating that I was to get into the chair with him.

Hope and doubt instantly warred within me. I was still buzzing from my last encounter, and I couldn't help but hope he meant to satisfy my discomfort. On the other hand, I had started with Kaelen. I really, really wanted Kaelen to pleasure me as I had pleasured him. More distressing than that thought, though, was the fear that he was only going to tease me more and I might 'slip'.

Swallowing against the reluctance in my throat, I placed a knee on either side of his hips and settled on his lap.

"That's not what I said, is it?"

I stared at him blankly, searching my mind, and finally remembered he had said on my knees. I pushed upward. Reaching for the tie at my throat, he pulled on it, releasing the bow and then shoved the sleeves of the sheer robe down my arms. He lifted his hands, cupping a breast in each and plucking at my nipples until they stood erect. He settled his hands on my waist then, pulling me forward until my breasts were inches from his face. I caught my breath as he opened his mouth. It wasn't his mouth that closed on the tip, though, but his teeth. He bore down slowly on the distended tip and then stripped it with his teeth. My nipple exploded with sensation closer to pain than pleasure. I gasped, began to shake as he raked it over and over with the edge of his teeth carefully applying just enough pressure to keep me teetering between pleasure and pain.

I was already feeling weak and faint before he turned his attention to my other nipple. Again, using only the edge of his teeth, he plucked at that nipple, pinching it and raking it just hard enough that it seemed to get more sensitive and more swollen each time. The restriction of the bustier on my ribs didn't help my desperate attempts to drag in a decent breath of air.

I moaned when he turned his attentions to tormenting the first nipple again, this time sucking it so hard I felt my belly quiver and hot moisture flood my sex. My legs began to quiver with the strain of holding myself up. I felt faint with the heat swirling through me, faint with breathlessness.

I had begun to make little whimpering sounds I was hardly aware of by the time he stopped, and I didn't know

if I was glad he had stopped, or very, very sorry. Every
nerve ending in my body felt as if it was on fire.

He stroked his hands downward along the curve of my
hips and then around me to cup the cheeks of my ass,
digging his fingers into the cleft. Slipping down in the seat,
he lifted me, thrusting my hips forward. An electrifying jolt
went through me as he caught my clit between his lips,
tugging at the painfully swollen nub in a way that sent
shockwaves of lava pouring through my veins and seemed
to suck all of the air out of the room. Clutching desperately
at the back of the chair, I struggled to suck in a breath as he
closed his mouth over it at last and began to suck it with a
feverish zealous that made my eyeballs roll back in my
head, left me gasping hoarsely in an effort to breathe.

I thought I would faint with the pleasure of it, die. My
body, already teased and allowed to cool twice,
skyrocketed toward completion. I groaned, struggling
against it, fighting to reach it. I was nearly there when it
abruptly flickered through my frying brain that I wasn't
allowed. I had to announce it and beg permission.

I didn't want to. I had a bad feeling permission would be
withheld.

I struggled with the consequences for several moments
more and finally gasped out the words I didn't want to say
in the worst way. "I'm … I'm … coming!"

He lifted his head abruptly. "Did you cum?"

I groaned, shuddering at the painful throbbing of my clit
as it screamed at being abandoned so abruptly. "No," I
gasped shakily, shivering now as the heat wafted off my
burning body.

"You are not permitted to cum."

I swallowed with an effort, but the tension had already
begun to ease. I dragged in another shaky breath just as he
closed his mouth over my clit again. My belly clenched
painfully at the fresh assault. Fire coursed through me. I
realized I had only thought my nerve endings were frying
before. Now, as he suckled the nearly painfully sensitive
bud, I began to feel as if fire ants were stinging me all over.
I groaned, squeezed my eyes tightly, trying to focus my
mind on something else.

I couldn't. I could feel my body gathering to take the leap despite my struggle to hold it at bay. "May I?" I gasped out desperately.

He stopped again, allowing me a moment's respite. "No."

I groaned as he plucked at the painfully swollen nub again, sucked it.

"That's enough, Gareth!"

A jolt went through both of us at the sound of that implacable voice.

I hadn't heard Kaelen enter the room, but that was hardly surprising considering my heart felt as if it was going to explode and had been pounding against my eardrums deafeningly.

Gareth lifted his head to stare at his brother. I was only peripherally aware of it, however. It was all I could do to hold myself up any longer.

After a moment, Gareth shifted upward in the seat again. As he did, he shifted me downward until my legs slipped from the seat of the chair. I was too wobbly to actually catch myself, but he didn't release me until I had settled on my knees. I watched him dully as he unzipped his pants and pulled his cock out, but I didn't need to be told what to do. I'm not sure I would've listened if he had informed me I wasn't to have it.

My brain was still frying. My body was on fire. I had a mindless need to have a cock in me, and I wasn't particular, at the moment, where. I opened my mouth as he speared his fingers through my hair and guided me to him.

He was definitely Kaelen's brother, I thought dizzily as his flesh filled my mouth!

"Suck me," he ground out.

Ecstasy flooded me as I took him into my mouth and began to suckle him as greedily as he had me. I was burning up, fevered. I needed release. I pulled and sucked on him with all that need boiling inside of me until he was shaking all over, groaning as incessantly as I had been. His hands tightened abruptly against my skull, holding me still for a split second and then he uttered a choked groan as his seed began to spill into my mouth. I almost came with the powerful surge of pleasure that flooded me. I sucked at him hungrily until I had drained him and his cock went flaccid in my mouth. I would have continued to suck in desperation if he hadn't finally pulled away from me.

I sat back on my heels, gasping for breath, still aching all over with the need thrumming through my veins.

"You have permission to go up to your room and rest for now. You'll be serving us luncheon in the dining room," Kaelen said, his voice even but threaded with anger. "Don't change."

He looked away when I finally lifted my head to look up at him. Turning, he strode to the door and went out. I stared at the door blankly after he had left. My jaws were aching from sucking the two brothers off, but my whole body was on fire, throbbing painfully with disappointment. After a moment, realizing I had been given an order, I got up and headed upstairs, leaving my robe on the floor at Gareth's feet.

Dev was leaning against the banister as I made my way down the hall on wobbly legs. He watched me through narrowed eyes as I drew nearer. Catching me around the waist as I passed him and mounted the first stair, he halted me, pulled me to him, and sucked one of my throbbing nipples into his mouth. An almost painful shaft of pleasure shot through me at the tug of his mouth on my swollen nipple. My knees threatened to give out. When he had sucked on it till I lost my breath, he released the first and caught the second. That time there was more pain that pleasure, but my sex still went wet at the heat that scoured my insides. He slipped his hands down from my waist and over my buttocks as he suckled the tip and finally released it. Watching my face, he slipped one hand down my belly and flicked at my swollen, exposed clit, sending another jolt through me.

He hesitated then, and I could see he was debating countermanding the order for me to go upstairs, but finally he dropped his hands and stepped away.

Thoroughly shaken, so weak I wasn't even certain I could make it up the stairs, I climbed them with a great effort and made my way down the hall to my room. Once I had closed the door, I collapsed on the bed. Every nerve ending in my body was still smoldering, sizzling as if I could still feel the touch of their mouths and hands on me. I ached with the need for fulfillment in a way I had not only never experienced, but never considered possible. I had almost felt like scoffing when Kaelen had said I was not allowed to cum without permission because I had been certain then that it wouldn't be a problem for me.

I could see right now that it was going to be a *serious* problem.

They were all attractive men, and I was still confused as to why I was so hot I felt as if I was on fire. My breasts had always been sensitive but not so sensitive that teasing them could arouse me almost to the point of orgasm. I was lucky if I warmed up enough to have a possibility of climaxing after penetration. Giving head had certainly never been a turn on for me, and if my ex had cum in my mouth, I wouldn't have given him any head again.

I found it hard to accept that it had been so hot and exciting just because I had been ordered to do it. There was no denying I had found both Kaelen and Gareth very attractive even before they had driven me half out of my skull with their teasing, and certainly Gareth's determined assault on my clit had been enough to make me cum, but I had been the next thing to frantic before he had gotten that far. I had been so ready I had almost cum the moment he had started.

I didn't even think it was the fact that I had been made to wear this 'fuck me' outfit that left my most sensitive areas exposed.

It was undoubtedly all of it together, though, and the fact that I wasn't allowed to cum only made me want to that much more.

If this wasn't their idea of punishment, I was pretty sure I didn't want to know what the 'punishment' for not obeying was going to be like because this was already hellish, and I knew damned well the other three were going to expect much the same. I rolled onto my back after a while, staring up at the drapery canopy above the bed and trying to will my body to cool down. It wasn't easy when every current of air that wafted over me brushed my nipples and my sensitive nether lips like a caress.

The straps were digging into my outer lips, too, restricting blood flow and making everything else ache that much more. I shifted, trying to get comfortable, but no position

seemed to ease the ache, either there or in my rectum ...
which I couldn't get my mind off of because of the plug.

The plug Kaelen was going to replace with a larger plug.

My belly clenched.

I hadn't even been here half a day and I was already
miserable.

Closing my eyes, I sought calm. My body ceased to throb
quite as uncomfortably as it had at first, but it didn't return
to 'rest'.

Finally, I got up, kicked the heels off my feet, and
explored the room.

There were scarves tied around each of the four posts of
the bed, I discovered, and I knew the moment I looked at
them that they weren't there merely to hold the drapes.
Feeling my belly shimmer, I turned away from the bed and
moved to the armoire. The wardrobe inside was in a variety
of colors, but I could see at a glance that each and every
garment was pretty much like the thing I was already
wearing, designed to offer me for their pleasure rather than
to cover me.

Closing the doors again, I glanced at the bedside cabinet
that Kaelen had pulled the plug from and finally yielded to
curiosity. There were three more plugs I saw in dismay,
each about twice the size of the one before. The largest was
the size of Kaelen's cock.

Shivering, feeling oddly more turned on by that discovery
than repulsed, as I was sure I should be, I closed the drawer
again and looked around, wondering if I actually wanted to
know what else the room contained.

I did, and I didn't.

It seemed inescapable that whatever I found was meant to
be used on me, and I was still torn. I didn't actually want
any surprises, but I wound never have known what the plug
was for before Kaelen had shown me. The chances were I
wasn't going to be able to figure out any other toys either,
and it might just shake my nerves worse than they were
already.

I looked anyway.

And mostly I was mystified, as I'd expected I would be,
but along with the pangs of fear of that discovery sent
through me were currents that were definitely erotic.

I was so busy checking everything out that I was nearly late for luncheon. Galvanized when I saw the clock hands nearing noon, I slipped the heels on again and headed downstairs, wondering where the kitchen was, and the dining room. No one had enlightened me. I had just been told to appear and serve.

I found the dining room easily enough. The men had gathered there, and I could hear them talking. Resisting the temptation to move close enough to tell what they were talking about, I moved further down the hall, knowing the kitchen would almost certainly adjoin the dining room and wondering abruptly if I was just to serve or to prepare.

And if I wasn't supposed to prepare, who was going to be doing that?

And was the cook going to pass out when he or she got a good look at my outfit?

Chapter Three

I peered around the door when I discovered I had found the kitchen at last. To my relief, it was empty. I went in, wondering what I was supposed to do about serving their luncheon and discovered there was a delivery box on the huge island that stood in the center of the room. Inside the cardboard box were a number of other boxes, these of the Styrofoam variety, and bags.

I took them out one by one and examined the contents, discovering they had ordered Chinese. It didn't appear to be individual meals, and it occurred to me anyway that Kaelen had probably not meant for me to carry the boxes in and toss them down on the table.

The food was still warm, but not hot, so it had either been delivered a good bit earlier or the delivery place was slow. Either way, I doubted I would get good marks for serving tepid food. After searching the cabinets, I pulled out some dishes to transfer the food into and looked around for a microwave.

I finally discovered it was one of the double ovens set in a sort of alcove several feet from the main cooking area—which was a huge, restaurant style stove with two built in ovens, warming ovens, a grill and griddle and four burners. Awed, I would have liked to simply stare at it and lust over it, but was already running late. Shoving a platter in to heat, I went back to collect plates, assuming the table hadn't been set either since I was pretty sure there was no one in the mansion besides me and the gang.

Conversation stopped altogether as I carried the plates into the dining room.

I discovered then that it was more of a breakfast room— had to be. It was a large room, but not by the scale of the house, and the table was only big enough to seat six. I imagined a mansion like this must have a formal dining room that would seat a good sized dinner party.

"Where's your robe?"

It was Kaelen that spoke, and I stopped instantly, sending him an uneasy glance as my mind raced around for the answer. I reddened as I remembered that Gareth had removed it and I had left in on the floor of the parlor.

"I like her better without the robe."

I glanced from Kaelen to Gareth. There was an undercurrent between them, but I wasn't sure if it was anything more than a typical sibling dispute. I set the dishes down. "I'll go get it."

"I agree with Gareth. I like her better without it," Dev spoke up.

I glanced at Kaelen again, wondering which one of them I was supposed to yield to when both Gareth and Dev had disagreed.

Kaelen, I saw, was looking at the others. Finally, he merely nodded. "Forget the robe."

I could see he still didn't like it, but I wasn't sure why. The robe didn't really cover me. If he was worried about the doubtful hygiene of having a half naked woman serving them it seemed to me he should have suggested I get dressed, not informed me to come as I was—which he had.

But maybe he was irritated because it seemed the majority had opposed him and he just didn't like being opposed?

I picked the dishes up and began to move around the table, setting one before each of them. Chance stroked my buttocks as I leaned to set his plate down. I glanced at him, but he didn't make any attempt to hinder my progress, and I moved down the table setting a plate before each man. Dev slipped an arm around my hips as I settled the last plate in front of him. Pulling me close, he plucked at my nipples until they were distended and my heart was fluttering uncomfortably fast as it occurred to me to wonder if he meant to take it further—in the dining room with everyone else watching.

Apparently his only objective, though, was to make them swell and jut outward, because as soon as he had tweaked them to the point where they were fully erect, he released me. I was shaking when I went back into the kitchen for the silverware.

Stopping long enough to pull one dish out of the microwave and put another in, I set the timer and gathered the silverware and napkins. Again I made the rounds, and as I did, first one and then another plucked at my nipples or stroked my buttocks.

I couldn't decide if it was just some sort of game to them, if they were trying to rattle me, or if they simply couldn't resist since it was so available. I supposed it was the availability, but it shot my concentration to hell. I dropped three glasses trying to get their beverages and all three shattered.

Biting my lip, certain they had heard the crash and breaking glass—wondering if it was going to be deducted from my pay—I looked around for a broom closet and found a broom and dust pan to clean up the broken glass.

No one touched me when I brought the drinks out.

I had to suppose it was because they didn't want me to accidentally drop iced tea in their laps.

It occurred to me about the time that I had heated up all the food that servers generally didn't eat with those they served, which was fortunate since it gave me the opportunity to fix a plate for myself before I had taken all the food in to them.

Not that I was terribly hungry. I had settled a good bit since the incident in the parlor earlier, but I was still over warm. The blood was still singing in my veins, low key now, but enough to keep me on edge, and Dev's teasing my already ultra sensitive nipples hadn't helped.

I fixed myself a plate anyway and carried the heated food in to set it on the table. Kaelen looked as if he might object, but he didn't say anything, and it wasn't until I had returned to the kitchen for the remainder of the food that it occurred to me that I might have been supposed to actually place the food on their plates.

Irritation flickered through me. I wasn't a trained servant, whatever they seemed to think. This was the way I served food in my own home. If it wasn't what they wanted, they would have to be more forthcoming. I couldn't read minds.

I was pretty good at reading expressions, though, and my instincts told me I had screwed up. To my relief, I saw when I made it back into the breakfast room that they were passing the platters around and helping themselves. I set the last two platters down and went back into the kitchen to eat my own meal.

I had only taken a few bites when Cameron pushed through the swinging door that separated the two rooms. He was holding an empty glass, I saw.

Sighing, I got up and retrieved the pitcher of tea from the refrigerator. He set his glass on the counter as I reached him then took the pitcher from my hands and set that down as well.

Catching me around the waist, he lifted me up and set me on the counter. I gasped in surprise as he did, and then sucked in another quick breath as my bare ass settled on the cold counter, and then winced as my weight pushed on the plug, sending vibrations along my nether channel that set my teeth on edge. Pushing my thighs wide, he examined me with his gaze and his hands. I groaned inwardly. If this was their idea of initiating me slowly into servicing five men, I wasn't going to make it through the first week.

I had known there would be some sex, but I had thought they were mostly just 'in' to having a submissive they could order around. I had expected to be picking up after them and fetching and carrying. I had not expected to be fondled until I was a mindless idiot and just about ready to start humping the bedpost.

I flinched when he began to fondle my breasts, knowing what was coming and completely unable to brace myself. Unlike Gareth, Cameron was gentle, and I still went up in flames the moment I felt his mouth close over my nipple, felt the heat of his mouth and the gentle suction. He pulled at it endlessly, flicking his tongue over the already excruciatingly sensitive bud until I was shaking all over and right back up at the peak, teetering toward climax and unable to reach it.

If he touched my clit, I thought wildly, I was going to cum, and then I was going to find out what Kaelen had meant about punishing me.

And I *knew* I didn't want to find out what that was like if this wasn't their idea of punishment.

I was 'saved' as he finally released the breast he had been tormenting by the opening of the kitchen door. Dev folded his arms and leaned against the opposite counter, apparently with the intention watching.

Cameron didn't seem too keen on being watched.

I found my voice with an effort. "Did you need something?"

Dev didn't care for me asking. He sent me a 'look', one of those chiding expressions I had learned already from

Kaelen that meant I hadn't behaved as I was supposed to. "You're not to speak unless spoken to."

The comment pierced the erotic high Cameron had given me. As I had suspected, it was yet another rule that they had forgotten to mention. I wondered if they were going to get together in the evening and review just how many times I had stepped out of submissive role. If they did and they started counting points against me, I was going to be in trouble.

"We're ready for desert," he continued when he saw he had rendered me speechless.

I blinked at him, searching my mind for something that had been in the delivery box that had looked like desert. I had emptied it, though. I knew there wasn't a desert in there.

That comment effectively distracted me from the first one, though.

Cameron helped me off the counter and apparently took pity on me. After studying my look of confusion for several moments, he said, "You."

That wasn't very helpful. Me, what, I wondered?

A slow grin curled Dev's lips. "Chance, Cameron, and I haven't had our head today. You're to come into the breakfast parlor and take care of that."

Shock wafted through me at that announcement. I'm sure I still looked bewildered as the two men escorted me back into the parlor. Dev led me back to his place and released my arm, settling in his chair and unfastening his pants. I could feel all eyes on me, but I couldn't bring myself to look around. Instead, I got down on my knees.

Dev was only semi-erect, I discovered, but he 'blossomed' even as I reached to grasp him. The circumference of his cock was somewhat less than either Kaelen's or Gareth's. I knew this because my fingers didn't meet on either of theirs and they did on his, not because I was in any condition to perform accurate calculations in my head. He was somewhat shorter, too, I thought. Not by a hell of a lot, but I discovered it was a little easier to take his cock into my mouth and I could take more of it.

Either my technique didn't turn him on as much as it had the brothers, or the fact that we were being watched distracted him, or he was just stubbornly holding out on me. My jaws were aching by the time I had managed to bring him off and so were my knees and back.

And I was still keyed up and ready to explode, my needs overshadowing even weariness.

Chance, poor man, was no more than average, not that he had any reason at all to be self-conscious, except that, compared to his friends, his average six inches looked small. He was also either far more sensitive, or far hornier, or far less able to hold his seed. Or maybe he had been worked up by watching me bring Dev off? Whichever the case, he was so excited that he ejaculated within moments of my first experimental suckling on his cock.

Relieved, I got up with an effort and moved to Cameron. To my surprise, he caught me around the waist when I stopped in front of him, turned me around, and pulled me down on his lap. Almost as if it was a signal, the other men got up and wandered casually from the room—except Chance, who staggered out a little drunkenly. Kaelen paused in the doorway as he was leaving and turned to fix Cameron with a look I had trouble interpreting. "Remember the agreement."

I thought he was talking to me at first, but Cameron nodded.

Kaelen flicked a glance at me and left without another word.

What agreement, I wondered?

Almost as if he could read my mind, which probably wasn't a great feat considering I was baffled and it probably showed, Cameron dragged me back against his chest and covered my ear with his mouth, sucking on it and bringing an eruption of goose bumps that made my poor nipples tighten painfully. "Not today, baby," he murmured when he had ceased teasing my ear and reached around me to cup and massage my breasts, plucking at the engorged nipples, "but you *will* cum for me."

I wasn't so sure it wouldn't be today, because I was in a bad way. I deduced from the comment, though, that there had been some agreement between them that I was to wait to have my pleasure—which I had already figured out. I just hadn't realized it was something they had decided between them. More importantly, it was some relief to

realize they planned to allow me to cum at some point, that
the torment wouldn't be endless.

That settled in my mind, my thoughts turned to my
current dilemma, and I wondered why Cameron and I had
been left alone. The others seemed to like watching as
much as they enjoyed participating, or at least almost as
much. Was Cameron just different, I wondered, or did he
have a reason why he didn't want to be watched?

The thought that leapt most immediately to mind was that
he was self-conscious and that led me to suspect it was
because he was less well endowed than his friends. Under
the circumstances, it seemed a reasonable supposition. Of
the five, Cameron was the smallest. I doubted he was much
more than five nine or ten and the others were at least six
foot tall. His build was more wiry than muscular, though he
was certainly not either skinny or weak. He had lifted me
straight up from the floor and set me on the counter, and I
was no frail little thing.

The mental exercise didn't distract me a good deal from
what he was doing, and not at all after a few moments. His
touch was unhurried, but I could feel tremors running
through him and that communicated itself to me as high
arousal even though he seemed in no great hurry to get me
on my knees to service him.

His cock was hard. I could feel it digging into my
buttocks.

He urged me to stand after a few moments. I turned to
him, expecting he was ready for me to suck him off.
Instead, I discovered that he had stood, as well. Leaning
over the table, he used one arm to clear a spot, grabbed me
around the waist, and settled me on the table top.

His gaze held mine as he slipped his hands down my
thighs and finally grasped my ankles. I leaned back as he
lifted them, finally going onto my elbows for support as he
placed my heels on the edge of the table. Anxiety smote
me. I had cooled somewhat, but not nearly enough I feared
to hold back if he decided to tease my clit.

Mentally, I braced myself the best I could for the
onslaught, trying to focus my mind on something else,
anything else. It was ironic that I had spent most of my
marriage struggling to focus on the sex act so that I could
get something out of it and now found myself, in the course

of less than a day, having to fight to get my mind on something else to keep from coming.

He stroked my legs from hip to ankle again and again. Finally, he lifted one leg, pushed the slipper off and brought my foot to his mouth. I stared at him, mesmerized, feeling my belly jumping and twitching even before he opened his mouth to suck my toes. The effect on me wasn't at all what I had expected. I had very sensitive feet, sensitive to the point that I generally disintegrated into helpless paroxysms of laughter if anyone touched them. I was completely unprepared for the bolt of fire that shot through me. Moisture flooded my sex, but I was too enthralled by the effect he was having on me to entertain any anxiety about the fact that my ass was on the dining table.

I could hardly catch my breath as he slowly savored my toes, flicking at them with tongue. He moved, after a few moments, along my foot, raking his teeth along the sensitive instep and then upwards along my calf. By the time he started up my inner thigh I thought I was going to pass out from oxygen starvation. I held my breath as he reached the apex of my thighs, expecting him to begin to tease my cleft, certain I would explode the moment he touched me. He hovered over my aching clit a moment, his harsh breaths steaming me there, then he moved to the other thigh and wound his way downward until he had sucked the toes of my other foot.

He settled that foot on the table again, studying my face for a long moment, his blue eyes glazed and glittering with the needs I could see were nearly as powerful as my own. He swallowed thickly when his gaze finally moved to the pink, swollen lips of my sex. "Just a taste," he said hoarsely, leaning down.

I groaned as the heat of his mouth covered me, blackness and stinging sensation covering me at the same time. The movement of his mouth and tongue were savoring rather than voracious, but it made my heart slam against my ribcage painfully, brought me nearer to passing out. "Cameron!" I gasped shakily. "I can't … I can't...."

He lifted his head. "Just a little more, baby. You taste so good."

I gasped, groaned, shook all over as he plucked gently at my clit and sucked. I was near to weeping with a mixture of relief and disappointment when he finally stopped and straightened. Lowering my legs, he drew me from the table to stand. To my surprise, he pulled me against him, slipping his arms around me and holding me while he stroked my back almost soothingly.

I was still shaky when he released me and sat down in the chair, but I had regained some measure of control. I went down on my knees as he unfastened his pants and unzipped them.

The thing he dragged out of his pants was a monster. A shock wave traveled over me as I reached to take it in my hands, wondering how the hell he had managed to hide something that big. It wasn't purely imagination, and it wasn't a trick of the eyes due to a comparison between his slight form and the cock he presented me with. I couldn't close my hand around it, not even close. I was doubtful I could get my mouth around it without unhinging my jaws.

I was eager, though, so eager I was far more interested in getting him in my mouth than massaging him as Kaelen had taught me. My jaw popped as I covered the cock head with my mouth. I sucked it eagerly, realizing even as I did that I wasn't going to get much more than the head in my mouth, and there was a *lot* more than head.

Almost reluctantly, I gave up the meat I had been sucking on mindlessly and began to massage him. I used two hands after a few moments when I saw that I couldn't cover enough territory with one to do more than irritate him. Tremors of need were wracking him even before I began. It turned me on that he was so aroused from touching me, encouraged me to work feverishly to please him. He groaned raggedly from time to time, shifting in his seat as I alternated between massaging his cock and struggling to engulf as much of it as I could in my mouth to suckle it.

Discomfort didn't enter my mind. I was so aroused I was completely focused on my newest toy, ravenous for the taste of him, desperate to suck his seed from him. When he finally uttered a guttural groan and yielded his seed, my body convulsed half-heartedly with pleasure. It was enough regardless to give me boundless enthusiasm, and I stroked and sucked at him until he could give me no more.

I had climaxed, I realized guiltily when I sat back on my heels at last, huffing for breath. It hadn't been much of a climax when all was said done, but my body had reached a surfeit of what it could take in the way of stimulation and knocked the edge off.

I hoped Cameron had been too caught up in the throes of his own release to realize it. Something told me from the way he looked at me that he suspected. He said nothing, merely drawing me up onto his lap and nuzzling my neck appreciatively as he cuddled me. He leaned back after a moment and studied my face, stroking a shaking finger along my jaw and then tracing the curve of my lips. "Something tells me," he said huskily, "that we're all going to be a sorry lot that we agreed to no kissing. I know I am."

I swallowed convulsively. Until he said it, I had forgotten that that wasn't on the list of things I had agreed to. The disappointment I felt in that moment was tremendous. Kaelen, I remembered, had nearly forgotten himself and kissed me earlier.

I had never especially *liked* kissing, though. I had way more experience in that aspect of petting than anything else, and I was only relieved when my ex finally reached the point of total disinterest in it because I was revolted by his sloppy wet kisses and irritated at his attempts to throttle me with his tongue.

I had very deliberately skipped checking that box, not just because I disliked the kissing, but also because it seemed too intimate. I had figured I could divorce myself from pretty much all of the rest, let them slobber over any of other part of me, or plow their cocks into me and, if I had to, count dollar signs. Kissing was a lot harder to ignore.

He frowned when I didn't respond, making me aware, finally, that he had expected one even though he hadn't couched it as a question. His arms loosened after a moment, and he helped me from his lap. "The afternoon's yours to do pretty much as you please. We won't expect anything in particular until this evening. I'd suggest you rest up, though," he said with a touch of amusement that made me distinctly uneasy. "Watch TV, read a magazine, explore the house if you like. The cook and maid will be in to clean up the kitchen and breakfast parlor shortly. You'll avoid these rooms—and Kaelen's office is off limits—but you can go anywhere else you like."

I felt badly that I had unintentionally snubbed him, but I firmly tamped the discomfort. I had wanted him to kiss me, I realized, almost as much as I had wanted Kaelen to kiss me earlier. That wasn't a good thing.

I was an employee, I reminded myself firmly as I left the breakfast parlor and returned to the kitchen to stare at the food I hadn't had the chance to eat. It was cold, of course. I heated it up and ate a little more, but I wasn't really hungry.

The little climax I'd had might have been something I would probably have congratulated myself over before I had arrived at the mansion, but it had been more like an interrupted sneeze than any real relief. My body wasn't screaming anymore, but it certainly wasn't appeased, not by any stretch of the imagination.

I worried that Cameron had noticed and might tell on me. He didn't seem like the type, but what did I know about any of them beyond the size of their cocks?

I discovered as I sought to entertain myself for the afternoon that 'anything in particular' only meant that I wasn't to be ordered to perform sexual acts with any of the men. It did *not* mean that they would keep their distance. I didn't see Kaelen and assumed he must be in the office Cameron had spoken of, but I ran into the others as I rambled around the mansion. It seemed to bother them if my nipples weren't at attention. If they did nothing else, they played with them until they were jutting again before they left me and wandered off.

I tried *not* to think about what they had planned for my evening, but it wove in and out of my thoughts, impossible to completely set from my mind. I was nervous about it. How could I *not* be? And yet I also had to face the fact that I was getting 'in' to this domination thing pretty heavily.

They seemed pleased with their choice. I still found that a little hard to swallow and finally decided it must be something about me that I wasn't aware of that they found a turn on. The fact that I was older, I wondered? It wasn't as if I was *that* much older than them, maybe a few years, but I couldn't help but wonder if that was part of it—the thought of dominating a woman who should've been mature enough and self-possessed enough to challenge them.

They weren't getting much of a challenge, though, because I might be mature, but I wasn't self-confident and even if I had been, my situation weakened my spine. Maybe if I hadn't been doing it for my children I would've been willing to say to hell with the money. I thought that was likely. But for their sake, I was willing to do whatever it took.

Fortunately, and it was probably the only break I had ever had, so far it hadn't been the horror I had expected. I was quaking, but not from fear and definitely not from revulsion.

I could've lied to myself, I supposed, and insisted that it was purely sacrifice, however willing, but it would've been a lie. Martyrdom hadn't entered my head since I had arrived.

Anticipation more nearly described my feelings even though I was still unnerved by some of the things I thought they might expect of me. The dread that stirred in me from time to time was the fear that my ex would find out and use this 'job' against me and anxiety about my children in general. I was allowed to call them each evening to talk, and I dreaded that the most. I hadn't really been away from them much, and they were clingy. The phone call was going to be an ordeal.

It turned out to be worse than I had expected. They were happy and excited at first, squabbling over the phone and both trying to talk to me at the same time about the kitten I had gotten for them to try to soften the blow of my absence. They commenced to whining and begging for me to come home, though, when it came time to hang up. It depressed me. I missed them, too, and I didn't like to think about the fact that my mother was tucking them in for me at night when that had always been my job.

I discovered when I had hung up that Kaelen had come into the room. I didn't know how long he had been standing there, but I doubted it had been more than a moment or two since he was standing in the doorway.

He gave me a searching look, but he didn't comment, which might've meant I was right and he hadn't overheard, and might also mean he just didn't want to get into any discussion that was too personal.

"You'll join us for dinner," he said after a moment, moving across the room to the armoire. Opening it, he selected what he wanted me to wear and carried it to the bed. "When I've bathed you, I'll help you put these on," he added almost absently, heading into the bathroom to adjust the water.

I stared at the empty doorway after he had disappeared, feeling blank. When he had bathed me? Maybe, I thought, I should have read up on submissives before I had come here? Not that I'd had any choice, but just as I had been in a constant state of arousal since my arrival, I had been in a constant state of confusion, and the surprises kept me off balance.

I didn't suppose, after a moment, that it really mattered whether I had read up or not. This game was being played by his rules, and it *was* whatever he decided it was.

I still thought it should have been the other way around. That I should have been told to bathe and dress him, but, on the other hand, there was no denying who was in charge.

They were a fastidious lot—which I was certainly glad of—and I supposed since they were sharing me they wanted assurance that I was just as cleanly minded.

Setting the phone on the bedside table, I got up and followed him into the bathroom. He helped me to undress, which was just as well, because I would have had a hard time getting out of the thing without help. To my relief and embarrassment, he had me bend over and removed the plug before he told me to get in.

I was still stinging with embarrassment when I settled and glanced at him.

My heart leapt into my throat when I did.

He was undressing, and that could only mean he planned to join me.

I tried not to stare, but I couldn't prevent myself from sneaking a few peeks as he calmly removed his clothes. I had known he was a big man, and I had thought he was well built, but I hadn't expected the finely honed body that emerged from the expensive tailored suit. It was patently obvious the man worked on his body. No way was all of those beautifully sculpted muscles au natural, though I didn't doubt he had been blessed with great material to work from. The shape and proportions of his body were nature's blessing, certainly. The wide shoulders and narrow hips, the long legs and big hands and perfect V from waist upward had been enhanced with rigorous workouts, but no amount of dieting, exercise, or even weight lifting could correct defects in proportions.

His cock was semi-hard when he mounted the steps and joined me in the tub. He settled behind me, pulling me between his thighs before he reached for the soap and washcloth. His touch was not impersonal. On the other hand, he also didn't seem to being going out of his way to arouse me.

He did, for all that. I rather thought he would have if he had only stood and watched me. The man exuded pheromones that drove me up the wall. Shivers I had trouble hiding or combating went through me as he scrubbed my back and shoulders and arms. When he moved his attentions to my front, though, is when I began to get really breathless. He paid special attention to my breasts—because they were so dirty, I supposed wryly—struggling to ignore the effect it had on me as he stroked and plucked at my nipples until rivers of fire were flowing through me.

He skimmed his hands downward after a while. My belly shimmied as his hands skated over it and clenched as he moved them down to place them between my thighs.

"Bend your knees," he said, his voice husky.

I gulped and pulled my legs up.

Slipping a hand behind my knees, he lifted my legs one at the time and moved them over his, settling my feet on either side of his thighs. He spread his legs then, pushing my feet sideways and spreading my thighs. Soaping the cloth again, he slid it down my belly and rubbed it along my cleft. He released the cloth after only a moment, though, and used his fingers, carefully tracing the area between my inner and outer lips and then right down the middle.

I sucked my breath in as he reached my opening and pushed one finger inside of me. Slowly, he sank his finger as deeply as he could reach and then just as slowly withdrew it. He pumped into me several times and finally withdrew his finger altogether. At least, I had thought that was what he was doing. Instead, he traced further down my cleft and touched my rectum. "Relax," he murmured near my ear and then promptly made that impossible by inserting his finger into that tight little bud.

I caught my breath and held it.

"Does that hurt you?" he asked, his voice rougher now.

I swallowed with an effort, thought about it a second, and finally shook my head.

As he had before, he pumped his finger into me several times and finally withdrew it. "Turn around in the tub and face me."

I moved away from him and turned, wondering what was to come next. I didn't have to wonder long. As I settled, I saw he had taken the shaving soap and razor. He scooted toward me, lifted one of my feet and placed it on his thigh with my knee bent. When he had smoothed the foam over my leg from my ankle to the tops of my thighs, he rinsed his hands and shaved my leg, lifting and turning it as necessary to reach all the way around.

I noticed his gaze flicking to my pussy more than once, though I wasn't certain if it was because he just liked looking at 'his pretty pussy' as he had said earlier or if it was because he suspected there had been some hair growth since that morning.

Apparently he did, because when he had finished shaving my legs, he made me stand up and sit on the edge of the tub. Spreading my legs, he examined me thoroughly with his fingers. I couldn't believe there would be stubble so soon, but he soaped me and shaved me anyway.

When he had finished, he rinsed the razor, pulled the plug, and stood up. I stood up, as well, but I discovered we weren't done. He twitched the shower curtains closed, turned on the shower, and shampooed my hair. His broad hands felt good against my scalp. I thought it might actually have soothed me except for the fact that I could feel his naked body brushing against mine or, more specifically, I could feel his cock brushing my ass as if sniffing out a nice warm hole to crawl into.

He seemed far more able to ignore his state of arousal than I was. Then again, he had gotten his cookie earlier, I thought irritably.

While I was rinsing my hair, he bathed, but absently. Most of his focus seemed to be on the water cascading over my body. He didn't seem really aware of that, however, or to notice that my focus was on his body as he scrubbed soap over his chest and arms and then dragged it down his perfect six pack to wash his genitals. I dragged my gaze from his cock with an effort and moved away from the shower head to allow him to rinse.

He followed me out within a few moments, taking up a towel and drying himself as he left the bathroom.

He had forgotten the plug I realized. Feeling a surge of relief, I finished drying and followed him.

Chapter Four

He had wrapped the towel around his trim waist, I saw, somewhat disappointed, but that beautiful upper body was still mine to stare at, and I saw his back looked as good as his chest.

He turned to look at me as he heard my approach and pointed to the bed. "Sit there."

A little surprised, I sat.

He picked up a bottle of lotion, filled his palms and smoothed the lotion over my legs. When he had finished, he told me to stand up and proceeded to lotion the rest of my body. It was almost relaxing. The massaging pressure of his hands did relieve some of my tension when he worked them over my arms and back, but somehow it had the opposite effect when he stroked them over my breasts and belly.

He left me to towel dry my hair when he had finished, and I heard the faucet as he washed the lotion from his hands.

He had the damned plug when he returned.

I glared at it with disfavor for a split second before I averted my gaze. Turning as I had before, I leaned over the mattress and presented my ass. He lubed the plug, spread my ass cheeks and shoved it home.

Swallowing against the discomfort, I straightened. He slipped a new bustier around my waist and fastened it. This one was a light aquamarine and more feminine looking that the leather one he had put on me earlier. It didn't have cups either, and it didn't have the shelf like top as the other one had had. This one merely ended just beneath my breasts allowing them more freedom of movement, I quickly discovered.

It was still uncomfortable, particularly since he cinched the waist in with drawstrings after he had fastened it.

The dreaded restraints came next. When he had adjusted them and tightened them until I winced, he caught my buttocks in his hands and pulled my hips forward. Fastening his mouth over my exposed clit, he sucked the bud until my knees gave out, and I would have fallen if he hadn't been holding me.

Steadying me, he stood up and finally released me.

Dazed, my mind a red haze of need, I watched him hungrily as he strode to the armoire again. He pulled something out that matched the bustier I was wearing in color. It was a dress ... of sorts. When he had helped me pull it over my head and adjusted it, I saw that the front was pretty much open from neck to hem. A broach had been sewn to the front, holding the edges together somewhere around my waist, which still left pretty much everything I had hanging out. The skirt, though, I thought, would cover my crotch, at least when I was standing still.

He handed me a pair of hose and watched me while I pulled them on and smoothed them. With a last order to leave my hair loose, he left me to comb and dry my hair and headed to his room to dress.

He hadn't said I was to 'do my face' but I never wore much make-up anyway, and I decided to take it upon myself to at least dab a little mascara on my lashes. Ordinarily, I would have put on a touch of blush, as well, but there seemed little point in that when my color fluctuated every few minutes anyway from the looks they gave me and the things they did.

Kaelen noticed. He met me in the hallway near the stairs. Detaining me, he tucked a finger beneath my chin and tipped my face up to inspect it. I met his gaze with a touch of trepidation but forgot everything as I did so. He had beautiful eyes. I would have killed for those long, thick, inky black lashes.

He swallowed audibly. "Acceptable," he finally said, breaking the spell.

I tried not to take that badly, but I couldn't help but wonder, again, why they had picked me of all the women that had applied. I began to think, though, that maybe I didn't really want to know. I had a feeling it was something about me that had nothing to do with sex appeal—not the way I would have liked, anyway.

I hated to think it might have been the sheer desperation in my eyes, but I still thought that might have been it—that and the fact that my background screamed inexperience with the world of 'kink'. Women married to one man for years had plenty of time to get used to being 'ridden' but they weren't married long if they had the tendency to look for outside experiences—which generally meant they weren't 'adventuresome'.

Instead of guiding me toward the parlor, he led me across the mansion to the game room I had discovered earlier. It was more of a pool parlor, I supposed, since the pool table was the focus of the room. The others, Chance, Cameron, Dev, and Gareth, were gathered around the pool table. Cameron broke just as we came in. Chance, Dev, and Gareth, who had been staring intently at the table, waiting for the break, turned to watch as we came in.

Kaelen led me to a stool and, grasping me around the waist, lifted me onto the seat. I hooked my heels on the rung below my feet. He promptly rearranged me so that I had one leg on either side. I didn't have to look down to know the new position had left my skirt gaping. I could feel the currents of air wafting over my exposed pussy. Even if not for that I would have known without looking because as Kealen stepped away, all of the men did, freezing in position and staring unblinkingly for several moments before they seemed to come out of their trance.

Kaelen crossed the room and propped against the wall to watch. His focus seemed to be on the pool table and the men playing, but since he had taken up a position directly across from me I wasn't sure he wasn't watching me—or at least watching the others watch me.

"How's the game going?" he asked.

Gareth flicked a glance at me. "I'm in the lead."

Kaelen's gaze moved to me for a moment.

Dev sent Kaelen a look I found hard to interpret. "You're not playing?"

Kaelen's dark brows rose. "I'm the host," he said coolly, but there was something in the way he said it and the look he gave Dev that made me think there had been some sort of challenge issued and repelled.

Cameron and Gareth exchanged a look.

I had never played pool. I found it fascinating to watch them, but I began to have the sense after a little while that there were undercurrents in the room that had nothing to do with the game they were playing. From time to time one or another of them would make some sort of challenging macho comment to another player, but the atmosphere wasn't relaxed like I would have thought would be the case with a group of friends playing a friendly game. They seemed a little more competitive than friendly.

There was an objective to this game, I finally decided.

I suspected I figured into it.

I wasn't sure why I got that impression. Mostly, after that first trance-like gaze I had gotten from the collective, they seemed to ignore me, but occasionally, as one game ended and another began, one would glance at me, study me for a long moment, and then look away again.

I was beginning to get uncomfortable from sitting so long when a strange man appeared in the doorway of the game room. "Dinner is served, Sir."

Nodding, Kaelen came away from the wall and moved toward me. As the men who had been playing pool broke off and moved to put the cues up, he helped me down from the stool and settled one hand on my back, just above my buttocks, escorting me from the room.

Gareth, Dev, Chance, and Cameron followed us, discussing points and games.

Kaelen guided me to the formal dining room, which I had discovered earlier while I was exploring the mansion. When he had escorted me to the chair at one end, he pulled it out for me. A little surprised, I sat.

It was a huge table, but I saw several leaves had been removed since I had seen it earlier. It was still long enough that when Kaelen took his seat at the opposite end he looked a long way off. Cameron and Gareth took the chairs nearest me. Dev and Chance, looking mildly annoyed, took the two seats on either side of Kaelen.

The table, I saw, was laid out formally. I stared down at the silverware, prodding my memory for the correct order I was to use the half dozen utensils.

The man who had summoned us from the game room came in with a bottle of wine and showed it to Kaelen. Kaelen nodded, and he proceeded around the table pouring wine for each of the diners. Surreptitiously, I adjusted the top of my dress as he neared me, trying to keep my breasts covered without being too obvious. The man very carefully refrained from glancing at my neckline, however, and moved on.

When he had left the room again, Kaelen glanced down the table at me and then looked at his guests. "How did the game go?" he asked casually.

Gareth sent me a smoldering look. "I came out in the lead."

Cameron flicked a glance at me before he turned to look at Kaelen. "Second place," he murmured.

Looking disgusted, Dev lifted his wine glass. "Third," he said, tipping the glass to his lips and draining it in one gulp.

Chance reddened and chuckled. "Guess I don't need to say anything. I never was worth a damn at pool."

I glanced at each of them as they spoke and finally looked at Kaelen, certain now that there were very definite undercurrents that baffled me.

Shifting in his seat, Kaelen produced a coin. He looked at Gareth pointedly. "Heads," he said implacably. Gareth frowned, but he didn't say anything. Kaelen flipped the coin, stared at it a moment, and looked at Cameron. "Call it."

"Tails."

Kaelen looked at Dev. "Heads." He flipped the coin again and looked at Chance.

"Tails," Chance said promptly.

Kaelen smiled faintly. "This just isn't your night, Chance. Heads."

Completely at sea, I stared at Kaelen and then at the others, trying to decide from their expressions just what was going on. It was useless. Aside from the fact that Cameron and Kaelen looked pleased with themselves, and the others less pleased, I couldn't tell what was going through their minds.

The server brought out a cart filled with dishes. Taking the shallow bowls off one at the time, he set a bowl before each of us and disappeared again. I stared down at the soup. It looked like lobster bisque. My stomach immediately leapt at the heavenly odor rising from the dish. I'd had almost no lunch, and the semen I had swallowed instead hadn't really been very filling. I was starving.

Lifting the soup spoon, I sampled the soup and discovered it was as delicious as it smelled.

"Excellent soup!" Chance said enthusiastically. "I should try to steal your chef!"

Kaelen flicked a vague annoyed look from Chance to me but smiled faintly. "I thought you already had."

Chance chuckled. "I did. He's seriously stuck-up, Kael. I don't know why you put up with him."

"Because he's the best."

Gareth glanced toward Kaelen sharply as if he had had a sudden thought. "Forgot ... I couldn't get those reports. They weren't ready."

Kaelen studied him for a long moment. He didn't look pleased. After a moment, however, he seemed to shrug it off. "Tomorrow," he said in a voice that brooked no argument.

Gareth looked as if he might argue, or at least say something else on the subject, but finally shrugged and returned his attention to his soup.

Cameron sent me an appraising gaze. "You're beautiful tonight, Annabelle," he said, his voice husky.

Startled, I glanced at him, feeling my face redden. No one, with the exception of my mother when she was really, really pissed off with me, called me Annabelle. I was actually surprised that he knew that was my full name. I didn't recall putting it on the application I had filled out.

I must have, I decided. Otherwise, how would he know that Anna was a short form for Annabelle?

I smiled at him uncertainly, pleased even though I strongly suspected he was talking about the clothes not the woman. "Thank you," I said hesitantly and then glanced at Kaelen, wondering if responding constituted speaking without being spoken to.

He was frowning at Cameron, I saw, but as if he sensed my gaze, he met it for a long moment. Finally, nodding slightly, he returned his attention to his dinner.

I wasn't sure if that was an approval or not, but it didn't really matter. I didn't feel comfortable about joining the conversation anyway, or trying to. They all knew one another. I didn't know any of them.

Gareth prodded Cameron with a comment about some incident they had both been involved in, and, as they fell to reminiscing, I studied the two beverage glasses in front of me—water and wine. I didn't particularly care for either one, but I wasn't sure I should indulge in the wine. I had never had a head for alcohol and rarely drank.

On the other hand, I was well aware of its properties.

I decided I would drink a little, just to take the edge off of my nervousness.

It took the edge off, all right. By the time I was halfway through the main course, I had discovered that Cameron and Gareth's anecdotes were hilariously funny.

Cameron took my wine glass and handed me the water. Since he winked at me when he did it, I decided he wasn't angry with me, but Kaelen didn't look terribly pleased. Subduing the urge to giggle at the look he sent me, I drank water for the remainder of the meal.

I was mildly disappointed when it ended. I was tipsy, and I knew it, but I had still thoroughly enjoyed the tales Cameron and Gareth had entertained me with of their boyhood together. Kaelen, Dev, and Chance had figured into a lot of them, but since Kaelen was older, I discovered, than Gareth by several years, he was 'away at school' during most of their wilder escapades.

Cameron helped me from my chair when we all rose to leave the dining room. Stroking my cheek lightly, he smiled at me. "Later," he murmured.

Surprised, wondering what he meant by that cryptic remark, I glanced up at Gareth as he came up behind me and settled a hand at the small of my back. Glancing at me, the others disappeared one by one, except for Kaelen, who waited by the door until Gareth had escorted me out and then followed us down the hall to the stairs.

Despite the wine, which had gone straight to my head and necessitated that I focus a good deal of my attention on walking without weaving, I began to get a feeling that something was definitely up as Gareth and Kaelen, without hesitation, led me up the stairs.

I was positive something was up when they escorted me to my room and went inside with me, closing the door.

Uneasiness moved over me, and I turned and stared at them a little doubtfully, feeling my belly tighten as they began to undress. Kaelen glanced at me as he removed his shirt. Frowning, he tossed it aside, moved toward me, and caught the hem of my dress, drawing it upwards and over my head.

I shivered as he discarded the dress and skated a hand down my arm.

"Nervous?" he murmured, his voice low but husky.

About what? I wondered, realizing abruptly that there was some sort of agenda here and someone had failed to give me a program booklet.

Gareth moved up behind me, skating a hand over my buttocks.

As I tipped my head to look up at him, he slipped his arms around me and cupped a breast in either hand, massaging them gently as he drew me back against him. He was naked. I felt the thrust of his cock against my buttocks, the prickle of his chest hair against my upper back.

He released my breasts after a moment, slipped a hand down to my waist, and urged me toward the bed. Shivering now with a mixture of nerves and anticipation, I climbed onto the bed. Gareth followed me, rolling me onto my back and nuzzling his face against my neck and the upper slope of my breasts. I felt the bed dip as he lifted away slightly and reached to cup one breast, tugging at the tip until it stood erect. Kaelen settled on the other side of the bed and rolled onto his side. Propping his head in his hand, he watched through narrowed eyes as Gareth plucked at my other nipple.

I knew where this leading. There wasn't enough alcohol in the world to blind me to that, short of drinking myself comatose. I just wasn't sure why both of them were in the bed with me.

Taking my arms, Gareth lifted them one by one and settled them above my head. Shifting downward then, he caught the nipple nearest him between his teeth and raked it just hard enough to send a jolt through me that felt like a bolt of electricity, frying nerve endings as it traveled through me. The fire they had built in me earlier had never died completely. It had only dwindled to smoldering ashes, and it took no more than the one touch to send me up in flames again.

I gasped, arching upward instinctively as he pulled on it. As I did, Kaelen leaned toward me and covered the other nipple, sucking on it hard and then plucking at it with the edge of his teeth as Gareth was doing. Twin bolts went through me then, shooting downward through my body to pool like fire in my sex. I gasped, moaned, writhed beneath them as they ignited my body into a blistering heat within moments. The wine I had drank was nothing compared to the euphoric drug that sent my mind reeling as I was bombarded with exquisite sensations so intense I couldn't catch my breath.

A hand stroked my lower belly and found my clit, teased it a moment, and then slipped lower along my thigh. I realized, dimly, that it was Kaelen as he caught the thigh nearest him and dragged it outward, opening my sex to him. His hand glided upward again along the inside of my thigh. This time he stroked my cleft, delving one finger inside of me as he found the mouth of my sex. I arched against the finger as he probed me, began to stroke me deeply.

"Kaelen!" I gasped desperately, unable to evade them. "I can't … I can't…."

He lifted his head, studying my face as he stroked me, and Gareth teased my nipple with his mouth and tongue and teeth until even my skin felt as if it was on fire.

"Only a little longer, baby," he murmured, leaning forward to suck a kiss along my neck. "Hold it for me."

To my relief, Gareth ceased to torment me and shifted into a sitting position.

Removing his finger, Kaelen told me to get up on my knees.

Dizzy, disoriented, I rolled over and struggled to comply. Gareth grasped me beneath the arms and dragged me over his lap, thrusting his cock against my lips. I opened my mouth over it mindlessly, aching all over, certain I was still to get nothing more than the opportunity to give them pleasure. Kaelen settled his hands on my waist, lifting until my hips were in the air. As he did so, Gareth speared his fingers through my hair, holding my head and guiding my mouth over his cock.

I felt something huge and rounded probing my cleft a split second before Kaelen aligned his cock with the mouth of my sex and thrust. If he hadn't been gripping my hips when he did so, he would have shoved me head first into Gareth's stomach. Pushing my legs further apart, he thrust again, wedging the head into my opening. I gasped around the cock in my mouth, struggling to focus on finessing Gareth's cock when my mind was entirely on the huge, engorged member Kaelen was fighting to force inside of me. My moisture coated the head as he pushed again, allowing him to slip deeper. He stroked me shallowly for several moments, coating his cock with my juices and finally, catching my hips firmly, rammed into me so hard I nearly strangled on Gareth's cock.

I felt Kaelen's flesh claim me completely, however, felt for several moments as if he was going to split me in two. I hadn't remembered him being so huge, I thought a little wildly. He leaned against my back, huffing hot, agonized breaths against the back of my neck. Tremors ran through him. Sweat had popped from his pores. I felt the dampness even through the bustier. "Jesus," he ground out hoarsely. "I need to take the fucking plug out."

My heart stammered at that. *That* was why I felt as if I was going to explode!

I lifted my head from Gareth, twisting to try to look at Kaelen.

Gareth guided me back to the business at hand. Dragging in a desperate breath, I covered him with my mouth again, sucked on his cock, began to stroke him with one hand as I supported my upper body with the other. Kaelen shifted upward after a moment. Very slowly, he began to withdraw, hissing between his teeth as he did so.

He paused when he had withdrawn all but the head, seemed to debate with himself.

Or maybe not.

The next time I went down on Gareth, Kaelen thrust deeply again. I groaned as he filled me almost beyond capacity, feeling my belly clench spasmodically as his cock stroked my inner channel. He pulled back as I lifted my head and then thrust again. Realizing he was matching his strokes to mine, I began to work my mouth and hands over Gareth more feverishly.

Kaelen moved with me.

"Now, baby," he growled as he leaned over me again. "Cum for me."

As if his words had opened a flood gate, I came with screaming intensity, groaning and suckling Gareth so voraciously as my body began to convulse that it seemed to set off a chain reaction. Gareth groaned, bucked against my mouth and exploded, shooting his seed down the back of my throat. Kaelen shuddered, stilled for a split second and began to pound into me so hard it nearly buckled my spine. Heat seared my channel as he spilled his seed. Groaning, grunting almost as if he was in agony, he leaned over me, jerking with each hard spasm of his climax.

He ground his teeth as he withdrew from me, collapsed on the bed beside me, and then rolled onto his back.

Weak in the aftermath of my own climax, I couldn't even do that much. The moment Kaelen let go of me, I collapsed where I was, gasping for breath with my face still in Gareth's crotch. He stroked my hair almost idly for a moment and then brushed it from my cheek, smoothing it.

Kaelen's arm landed on my back. His hand hooked around my waist, and he rolled me off of Gareth and onto the bed. I rolled limply, too weak even to attempt to control my body. His hand settled on my ribcage for a moment and then stroked downward over my belly and between my splayed legs. I moaned softly as his fingers brushed across my cleft. He hesitated, stroked it once more, and then brought his hand upwards again.

Levering himself up on one arm finally, he leaned toward me, sucked one nipple into his mouth briefly and then released it. "Don't wash up," he murmured, reaching to pat my thigh as he straightened resolutely. "Cameron's going to need the extra lubrication," he finished wryly and then rolled off the bed and headed to the end of the room where he had discarded his clothes.

I lay where he had left me, still trying to gather the strength to move, pondering the cryptic comment. As Gareth left the bed and collected his clothes to put them on, it finally all clicked together in my fried brain.

They had been jockeying for position in the game of pool, or rather order. The coin toss had determined the positions. Dev, Gareth, and Chance had gotten heads.

I had recovered enough to wonder if I should just stay in the bed when the door opened again and Cameron and Dev came in. Levering myself up on my elbows, I watched them as they undressed and moved toward the bed.

Cameron was far better built than I had expected. He was lean, hardly seemed to have an ounce of spare fat, but his muscles were well developed for all that. He was surprisingly hairy, I thought, for a blond. A thick, golden brown pelt covered most of his chest and narrowed to a trail down his ripped belly before widening again to form a nest for the beast that sprouted from his lower belly.

Dev was a good bit bigger, and also well built, but he didn't have the definition of any of the other men. He was obviously no weightlifter, despite the bulging muscles on his upper arms and his nicely shaped chest and legs. His body was purely a gift of nature, and it was a very nice gift.

I sat up as both of them climbed onto the bed on either side of me. Dev caught me around the waist and carried me down again, burrowing his face between my breasts and then up to one tip to suckle it. As sated as I had thought I was, my body stirred to life instantly, warming at the tug of his mouth and the stroke of his hand as he massaged my other breast.

I thought, at first, that Cameron had decided not to participate, but in a moment, I felt him grip one ankle. He lifted my foot to his mouth and began to suck my toes, one at the time. Heat traveled along my leg and went straight to my core, fanning the coals of my spent passion. My heart and lungs, which had barely returned to normal, began to labor again.

I lay as still as I could beneath their ministrations, savoring the feel of their mouths and hands on me, allowing my body to climb at will toward yet another pinnacle, though I seriously doubted I would reach it. I wasn't even certain if it was allowed. Kaelen had wanted me to cum for him, and I realized that might not carry over to this pair.

I dismissed the doubts, ready to enjoy it regardless, feeling far less harassed than I had before Kaelen had allowed me to cum. At least now I knew I wouldn't have to endure endlessly without fulfillment.

When Dev finally urged me to turn over and take him into my mouth, I was eager to do so. Positioning myself on my hands and knees, I stroked him, suckling his cock.

Cameron's hand skated over my bare ass, stroked me. Instead of feeling his member prodding me, however, I felt the rake of his teeth along one cheek. Goosebumps leapt to life all over me. I shivered at the awakening of thousands of tiny nerve endings that had lain dormant, working over Dev more and more enthusiastically. His breath became more and more labored as I stroked his shaft and testicles, sucked the head of his cock, and then the soft sack beneath, and then took him deeply into my mouth and sucked him again. And all the while, Cameron gnawed along my buttocks and thighs and calves and feet, making me hotter and hotter until I could barely be still.

Dev's hands tightened on my head as he reached his crisis. He hovered, tremors running through his body. I took him deeply into my mouth again and sucked him hard. Uttering a choked groan, he yielded up his seed to me, his hands tightening against my skull as he jerked and arched upward with the convulsions of his release.

Gasping for breath, I lifted my head when I had sucked him dry, falling limply to one side of him. As I flattened myself against the bed, Cameron moved over me, nibbling the patch of bare skin below the bustier. Pulling my legs apart, he shifted higher, wedging his hips between mine and nestling his engorged member against my throbbing clit. Uttering a sound of pleasure, I arched against him as he curled his hips into me, pressing his cock almost bruisingly against my cleft.

He nuzzled my breasts as he settled his upper body lower and then burrowed his face against my neck as he lifted his hips upward and caught his cock, stroking it along my cleft in search of the mouth of my sex.

It was as well he was getting sloppy seconds, I thought wryly as I felt the probe of his cock head.

Or maybe not.

I was so slick with my own juices and the semen Kaelen had bathed my channel with there was little resistance beyond the limitations of my flesh to expand to his girth. His first thrust embedded him deeply and left me gasping to catch my breath as his thick member filled me to the point of pain. I arched upward instinctively, driving him more deeply still and cried out as the head of his cock slammed into my womb and it convulsed. He stilled, nipping lightly at my neck, lifting his head to tease my ear with his lips and tongue.

The pain passed after a moment, and my muscles clenched around his shaft. He groaned as he felt them tighten around him even more. "I won't last three strokes if you keep that up," he murmured in a choked voice that was nevertheless threaded with wry amusement. "God, baby, you're so tight and hot."

Tight? I thought a little wildly. I was about to rupture with that anaconda he called a cock.

After a moment, he began to move cautiously, stroking my channel with slow, even thrusts. There wasn't an inch of my channel he missed. The moment he began to move he began to rub my g-spot and waves of pleasure rocked me. Gasping, moaning at the excruciating, intense pleasure, I moved in concert, trying to force him to increase the pace. "Cameron," I gasped out with an effort. "Cameron."

He shuddered, began to move faster in response to the desperation in my voice. I drew my knees up, matching him stroke for stroke.

"Annabelle," he groaned. "That's it, baby. Cum for me. I want to feel you cum."

My heart seemed to trip over itself. I groaned as I felt my body coil tightly as it prepared to explode with ecstasy, straining toward it, straining toward him. Clutching him tightly, I bucked as the first convulsion hit me, cried out at the force of it.

He shuddered, drove into me faster until I was screaming hoarsely with the wave upon wave of intense rapture that gripped me. Driving deeply, he went still, tensed all over, and then began to shudder and jerk as he climaxed with me.

We lay locked together in the aftermath for an endless time. I was barely conscious, and yet it warmed me to feel the weight of his body on me, satisfied me beyond the sense of complete satiation in the wake of my climax to feel his breath against my neck and the brush of his lips in appreciation.

I was more than half asleep when he withdrew from me at last and rolled away.

The closing door roused me. I thought at first it was Cameron and Dev leaving, but I discovered as I lifted my head to look that Chance had come in. Kaelen was with him. Heavy eyed with both weariness and satiation, I stared at them, resisting the urge to groan with reluctance this time.

Chapter Five

I couldn't arouse so much as spark of want to. I had been thoroughly satisfied twice already and was worn out, as well, but as Chance climbed into the bed with me I gathered myself to fake it the best I could, caressing his back as he aroused himself by stroking and fondling my body.

As he tugged and suckled energetically at my nipples and stroked my clit, warmth stirred to life again to my surprise and dismay. I hadn't realized until I felt the burgeoning of warmth that the lack of want to included any desire to *feel* any more desire. I was glad to know I wasn't frigid, as my husband had often accused me of being, but this polar opposite of my former self wasn't somebody I wanted to be.

It stirred anyway. I wasn't sure why. I was sure it wasn't a newly discovered facet of my inner self that I was terribly pleased with.

Kaelen made no attempt to join us. I had heard him approach the bed, expected that he would climb up on the other side. Instead, he merely folded his arms over his chest and watched—I thought I felt his simmering gaze, anyway.

Chance, I remembered as he pulled me on top of him finally and began urging me on a southerly route, was heads.

I wanted to rush through it in the hope that I could accomplish a climax for him without getting too stirred up myself, because I just didn't feel up to coming again, entertained a lot of doubt that I could. It was nothing short of miraculous as far as I was concerned that I had already cum twice, but I put that down to the teasing I had endured all day.

It seemed rather unfair to poor Chance, though. He had lost at pool and lost the coin toss. I felt guilty for even wanting to short change him, which was why I resisted his attempt to get me to give him head immediately. Instead, I lavished caresses all over his chest and belly with my lips and hands. His skin was smooth and silky and unlike the others, his chest and belly was virtually hairless. A narrow, thin patch of hair grew between his breasts and around each nipple. I teased his nipples, plucking at them with my lips until they puckered and stood erect, and then nipping at them carefully with the edge of my teeth as Gareth had a tendency to do.

He nearly came up off the bed the first time. Gulping, he settled back again, panting for breath and struggling to remain perfectly still while I teased him. When he began to move restlessly beneath me, I moved lower, sucking at little patches of skin and flicking my tongue over the spot to ease the sting. By the time I reached his cock, pre-cum had puddled at the tip and run down his erect shaft and he was wracked by almost continuous tremors.

He couldn't decide where to put his hands. He caught at me, clenched his fingers into me and released, stroked my shoulder and head.

Wrapping my hand around his cock, I sucked the head, lathing it with my tongue. He groaned, his hips coming up off the bed. He was a far more manageable size than the others. I could take his entire cock into my mouth almost to the root and close my mouth tightly enough around his girth to suck a blister. I took full advantage of the circumstance, focusing on using my mouth more than my hands, dragging on him with my mouth as if I could suck the cum out of him.

I think I did at that. Within moments he was lifting each time I went down on him, surging into my mouth eagerly. Sensing his nearness to release, I began to move faster, sucking him hard every third pass. I had managed no more than a half dozen or so strokes when he went rigid all over. Clamping his hands against my head as I drew on his cock with my mouth, he uttered a hoarse cry, shuddered all over, and then his cock began to jerk in my mouth as he came.

He went limp all over as I sucked the last of his cum, shuddered as I finished by licking and sucking at his limp member and finally released him and fell back on the bed, struggling to catch my own breath.

I fully expected Kaelen to move to the bed then and realized I had been waiting for him with more than a little anticipation. Instead, he shoved away from the wall and moved around the bed to the bathroom. I heard the water running.

Apparently Chance did, as well, and decided it was his cue to depart. He struggled out of the bed and headed to the pile of clothes he had left near the door. He didn't bother to put them on, however. He merely gathered them into a ball and let himself out.

Kaelen returned after a few moments and climbed onto the bed. Instead of initiating sex, however, he urged me onto my belly, and I felt his hands moving down the back of the bustier. It went slack. Slipping an arm beneath my hips, he lifted them upward until I was on my knees, unfastened the restraint in the back. The bustier fell off me as he released it and reached to remove the plug from my rectum. I gasped as I felt it slip out, shuddering.

He moved away for a moment and came back. Scooping me into his arms, he hefted me against his chest and carried me into the bathroom, mounting the steps to the tub and finally settling in the hot, swirling water with me on his lap.

The hot, swirling water relaxed me almost to the point of sleep. I felt pampered in a way I couldn't even remember ever being before, babied as he soaped a cloth and bathed me with measured strokes.

When he had finished washing me, he used his hands to rinse the soap away, stroking me long after he had removed the last speck of soap. Finally, he lifted me away from his lap and got out. I watched through half closed eyes as he dried himself briskly with a towel and finally reached down to turn off the whirlpool and release the water from the tub.

Catching my arm, he slipped his hand along it until he was grasping my wrist and tugged at me, urging me up. Sighing with reluctance at having to leave the nice, warm pool of water, I got up with an effort, wobbling slightly as I lifted my leg to climb out. He caught me around the waist, swung me out and settled me on the rug beside him. Grabbing a towel, he rubbed me down briskly, tossed it aside and caught my hand, tugging me back into the bedroom.

He stopped me before I could crawl into the bed, grabbing the edge of the comforter and flipping it back. Still naked and more than a little damp, beginning to shiver from the cool air, I climbed between the sheets and the comforter and settled with a deep sigh of bliss.

Kaelen climbed in, as well. Settling on his side against me when he had adjusted the cover, he propped his head in his hand, studying my face. I stared back him, wondering at his mood and his intentions as he lifted his free hand and splayed it lightly along my cheek. His palm was large, his fingers long and tapered. His hand covered the entire side of my face from ear to chin. For a long, long blink, we merely stared at one another. Finally, he transferred his gaze to my lips, watching almost as if transfixed as he lightly brushed his thumb back and forth across my lower lip.

Uttering a sound that seemed equal parts irritation and frustration, he moved his hand and rolled over me, shoving one arm beneath my shoulders. His mouth grazed my cheek lightly and moved to my ear. Shivers skated through me as he opened his mouth over it, sucking at the shell and then delving inside, tracing the intricate swirls with the tip of his tongue. I sucked in a sharp breath as the heat of his mouth and tongue invaded me, coursing along my veins like fire following a trail of gasoline and then bleeding outward through my pores and nerve endings. He moved along my cheek to my jaw, nipping at the bone beneath the surface with the edge of his teeth and then dipping below that hard line to explore my throat and the side of my neck.

With the tip of his tongue, he traced the hollow at the base of my throat and then my collar bone. I lifted my hands, splaying them along his shoulder blades, digging the tips into his flesh a little frantically as he wound his way downward with an odd mixture of fervor and indolence, seemingly in no great hurry to make much progress, and yet prodded by a hunger that compelled him to suck and lathe a trail of tingling love bites on every inch of my skin. Again and again, he moved from the top of my breasts, up to my ear, along my cheek to the corner of my mouth and then beneath my chin and along my throat until I was drunk with the heat fogging my mind, uncertain of which of us was shaking more.

By the time he moved to my breasts, I was near desperate to feel his mouth on me. He leaned slightly away from me, skating a hand down to cup and massage one as he caught the tip of the other breast between his teeth. I gasped sharply as he nipped at it, raked his teeth along the turgid peak as it flooded with blood. He suckled it as he ceased to massage my other breast and ran his hand down my body. Catching one thigh, he lifted it, insinuating a leg between mine, and then slipped his hand upwards to cup one buttock as he curled his hips, pressing his swollen member against my cleft.

Warm currents of desire swirled and eddied through me, pierced with shafts of exquisite heat each time he pressed against my clit or plucked at one of my nipples. I was long past any ability for thought by the time he reached between us and guided his cock along my cleft to the mouth of my sex, surging upward to engage our bodies. I arched to meet him, foiled by the awkwardness of our positions. He drew my thigh higher, shifted down and thrust upward again, sinking a little deeper.

Frustration filled me, hunger. I wanted to engulf him completely, to feel him deep inside of me. He taunted me, stroking me shallowly, inching a little deeper, but never reaching the spot where I needed to feel him. I moved restlessly against him, arching to meet him with every stroke, clutching at him, digging my fingers into his flesh.

Abruptly, he rolled with me until I was on my back, thrusting hard, claiming me completely. I gasped as quakes moved along my channel, my muscles clamping around his flesh frantically. "Anna," he breathed hoarsely against my neck as I lifted my legs and wrapped them tightly around his waist, using the leverage to engulf him even deeper inside of me. "Jesus, baby, you're so tight, so hot and wet for me."

The absurdity of being called baby by a man easily five years my junior was lost on me. The caress in his voice as he said it was all that registered beyond the need in his voice and even that was burned away from conscious thought as he set a rhythm that stoked the fire inside me higher and higher until I felt like I was on fire, burning from the inside out.

Dropping my feet to the bed, I curled my hips to receive his pounding thrusts, goose bumps erupting all over me as the new position angled his thrusts to strike me in just the right place to drive me toward release. He left off sucking at my neck and came up on his elbows, staring down at my face. "Cum for me, Anna. That's my baby," he murmured encouragingly as I let out a desperate gasp. As if my body was his to command, the moment he demanded it, my muscles seized and began to convulse with such exquisite pleasure it drew hoarse, ragged cries from my throat.

He changed the tempo of his pace as the convulsions subsided, but his thrusts were all deep, stroking that one spot with such pointed focus that my body seized again, harder than before. I screamed at the sheer magnitude of it, my fingers curling into claws, digging into him. He shuddered, missed a beat, and ground against me as he was caught up in his own release, uttering a long, low growl as his body convulsed, pumping his seed from him.

I floated downward as the paroxysms eased, dropping into complete oblivion. I only stirred once and that was when, sometime during the night, Kaelen moved away from me and left the bed. Rolling onto the warm spot where he had lain, I gathered a pillow to my chest and sought unconsciousness again.

Kaelen was heavy eyed when he came in and woke me the following morning. Barely conscious myself, I studied his expression dully, mildly disturbed by the heavy scowl he wore but completely unable to gather my wits enough to try to figure out why he might be angry.

When he went into the bathroom to run a bath, I collapsed face first on the bed again and was drifting toward sleep when he jerked the covers back and smacked me soundly on the ass. It stung, but it was the loud smacking sound that jerked me wide awake. I scrambled up, blinking at him owl eyed in an effort to focus my eyes. He jerked his head toward the bathroom.

Biting my lip to keep from groaning as my muscles protested, I clambered out of the bed and staggered into the bathroom, slamming the door behind me. I sat on the toilet with my eyes closed as I relieved myself and finally got up and climbed the stairs into the bath. A jolt went through me the moment I stepped in. The water was cold enough to snatch my breath from my lungs as I skidded and sat with a hard splash. I let out a yelp and shot upward just as Kaelen slammed the door open so hard it hit the wall and bounced back, his blood shot eyes rounded with alarm.

"C..c ...cold," I gasped through chattering teeth, wrapping my arms around myself.

He gave me a deadly look, stomped over to the faucet and turned the hot tap wide open, then turned on his heel and stalked out again, slamming the door harder than I had inadvertently slammed it. I stared at the vibrating door blankly for several moments and finally waded across the tub to squat in front of the tap where the water was marginally warmer. Soaping the cloth from the night before, I scrubbed myself off quickly, focusing mostly on washing my sex, which I discovered was uncomfortably tender after all the pounding the night before.

By the time I had washed my face and brushed my teeth, I was slightly more alert, but still felt far too fragile to summon more than a flicker of resentment over the fact that Kaelen seemed pissed off with me and I had no idea why.

Even that flicker died, though, as I left the bathroom and faced the lion in my den. He had already fastened the restraints between my legs before he remembered the plug. I had remembered it, but I nursed a hope he wouldn't and kept my mouth shut.

He sent me an accusing glare as glanced at the bedside table and spotted it. Unfastening the restraints he had just fastened, he stalked over to the bedside table and snatched the thing up, slathering lube on it. Biting my lip, I leaned over the bed as he headed toward me with it.

I supposed, reluctantly, that I must be getting used to it. It wasn't as uncomfortable when he thrust it inside me as it had been the first few times. I didn't especially *want* to get used to it, but I seemed to be.

Studying him as he knelt to fasten the restraints again, I decided that, maybe, he was just cranky because he wasn't a morning person. Either that, or he had just not gotten much sleep because he had kept me up half the night fucking, which the dark circles beneath his eyes seemed to suggest.

"You have two rest times," he said coolly as he finished and straightened. "Eleven to twelve, and three to five—in your room. If you choose *not* to return to your room, it will be assumed that you feel no need to rest. You'll serve luncheon as you did yesterday—the servants won't be in until late in the afternoon to prepare dinner—but I had the chef prepare the food so that all you'll need to do is warm it. Unless you're entertaining, you may do whatever you like with your time." His gaze flickered over me assessingly. "You are not allowed to cum today."

When he had left, I simply stared at the door for a time, frowning as I tried to puzzle through his behavior. He was not exactly a warm, open sort of man anyway from my short acquaintance, but he hadn't seemed prone to temper either. He had seemed more ... aloof, I decided, neither warm nor cold, just withdrawn. It still seemed odd to me that he appeared to be in a foul mood. I had been more thoroughly satisfied than I had ever been before in my life. I still felt that special glow ... except now it had dulled just a bit in the face of his grouchiness.

Dismissing it finally, I glanced down at myself. He had only helped me into a fresh bustier and left. I wanted breakfast. I was starving, but I wasn't so sure I should sit down at the breakfast table as I was.

On the other hand, Kaelen was pretty damned bossy, a man obviously accustomed to having his way. If he had wanted me to wear anything else, he would have chosen it.

Expelling an irritated breath, I left the room as I was, reflecting that I had at least satisfied the whole gang—twice—the day before and that it should hold them a while.

Contrary to that blithe assumption, I discovered that what I had done only seemed to be like pouring gasoline on a fire. All of them were awake. All of them were downstairs, and it seemed that all of them had their ears pricked for my appearance. The moment I stepped off the last stair and my heels clicked against the marble tile, Chance, Dev, and Cameron appeared in the doorway to the parlor. Gareth brushed past them, grabbed my wrist, and, after glancing at the three men now glaring at him, tugged me down the hallway toward the kitchen. The moment we cleared the door, he caught me around the waist and hoisted me onto the island counter.

Cold shot through my buttocks as my bare ass settled on the icy surface and heat shot from my breast downward to collide in a minor explosion in my belly as Gareth squeezed both of my breasts in his hands and caught one of my nipples between his teeth as if he meant to eat me alive.

I groaned as a tidal wave of desire washed over me, and Kaelen's last order flashed through my mind. I had been relegated again to teeth gritted endurance, except that now my body was much more reluctant to obey me than it had been the day before.

Luckily for me, Gareth was already wound up. As if coming in my mouth the night before had only teased him, he released my breasts almost at once and reached down to unfasten his pants and unzip them. His pants promptly slipped down his hips, but he scarcely seemed to notice. Catching my other breast in one hand, he teased that nipple as he had the first, reaching down to flick his finger over my clit and then delved my cleft and shoving a finger inside of me.

As good as his mouth felt on me, I hadn't actually had time to warm up, hardly knew which end was up. Frowning when he discovered I was barely damp, he worked his finger inside of me a moment and then changed tactics abruptly. Planting a hand on my breasts, he shoved me back, grasped my hips as I flattened out and yanked them upward to meet him as he lowered his mouth to my clit.

A jolt of fire went through me then.

Anything but that, I thought a little wildly, feeling blackness cloud my mind as my body shot from zero to sixty in two seconds flat as he fed greedily on my clit. I groaned, bucked against him, more interested in evading the torture of his mouth than embracing it. His head came up after a moment and he rammed a finger inside of me again. Discovering I was wet, he dragged me to the edge of the counter and pulled me upright. I slipped off the edge just as he aligned his cock with the mouth of sex, grunting as gravity helped him impale me on his shaft.

"Oh Jesus," he ground out as I wrapped my legs around his waist and caught his shoulders with my hands to keep from falling, enabling him to sink deeply inside of me. His arms tightened around me as he heaved several times, bouncing me up and down on his shaft. Grinding his teeth, he leaned against the counter, trying to get more leverage to take longer strokes. "Jesus, Anna, baby," he muttered in a litany as the goal eluded him and he could manage no more than short, deeply embedded strokes.

I bit down on his shoulder to contain a groan as I felt my body quicken in response to the pounding strokes against my g-spot, knowing any moment I was going to completely lose it. He beat me to it, uttering a hoarse growl as he came, biting the side of my neck and sucking hard as he ejaculated his seed into me in hot bursts that matched his convulsing thrusts.

He swayed weakly when his body ceased to spasm but managed to settle my buttocks on the edge of the counter. Huffing for breath, he nuzzled my neck appreciatively. "You feel so good, Anna, so good, baby. I wanted it so bad. I'll make it good for you tonight. I promise," he murmured gustily as he lifted his head at last and pressed his forehead to mine.

I lifted my eyelids with a great effort when he caught my head between his palms and pulled away to stare at my face. My heart was still thundering against my ribcage with the near miss, my body clamoring for the release denied me. He moved his lips over my face in nibbling kisses and finally paused with his lips barely a hair's breadth from mine. For a long moment, he stared deeply into my eyes. I held my breath, fighting the urge to close the distance and feel his lips on mine.

It wasn't rational thought that stopped me. It was the sudden flash of warning in my mind.

"Shit!" he ground out as if he had suddenly remembered that was off limits, pulling away from me so abruptly I nearly fell off the counter. He steadied me, straightened his shorts, and hitched his britches up over his hips, looking around a little vaguely as if he was surprised to discover we were in the kitchen. Striding toward the sink, he dragged his cock out and washed the residue of sex from himself, then grabbed a paper towel to dry off.

I watched him with a mixture of horror and unseemly amusement. When he had zipped his pants, he returned with a wet paper towel, dabbed at my nether lips, and finally handed the towel to me. As thoughtful as it was, I wasn't terribly comfortable cleaning myself in front of him. On the other hand, I didn't want to be dripping cum in the kitchen either.

"Hungry?"

I looked up at him in surprise and finally nodded.

His lips curled. "I make a fairly tolerable omelet."

Without waiting for a response, he began opening and closing the cabinet doors in a search for a bowl, finally dragging out a metal mixing bowl that looked big enough to mix a cake in. Keenly conscious of the use we had put the kitchen to I went in search of germ killer when I had finished cleaning up. It might only have been my imagination, but it seemed to me the room wreaked of sex, and I thought it likely the chef would have a heart attack when—if—he noticed it.

Gareth grinned at me, reddening faintly when he saw what I was about. Chuckling, he focused on hacking up the ingredients he planned to add to his omelet and finally dragged a carton of eggs out of the refrigerator. He used half a dozen, dropped shells and egg whites all over the counter top and the floor, burned the first pats of butter, tossed the frying pan and burned butter into the sink and grabbed another pan. By the time he flipped his omelet onto a plate, the room no longer wreaked of sex. A dull haze of smoke drifted through the room about head high, and the entire room looked as if a tornado had swept through it.

Grinning triumphantly, Gareth cut the omelet in half, divided it onto two plates and, settled both at the kitchen eating counter. I grabbed glasses, filled them with orange juice, and found forks before I joined him.

He watched me until I had tried the first bite. "Good?"

I smiled at him. "Very good," I responded, meaning it.

He frowned as he took a bite of his own, and I wondered if he had discovered a piece of egg shell in it. "You can talk, you know," he said without looking up at me.

I stared at him as he looked up at me, struggling with the uneasy feeling that he was, for reasons completely unknown to me, trying to sabotage me. I cleared my throat uncomfortably after a moment. "Kaelen said I wasn't allowed," I responded finally instead of pointing out that, from what I could tell, the ground rules had been designed with two purposes in mind. One, to make certain I behaved like a proper submissive, and, two, to keep the relationship in it's proper place. Friendliness was liable to encourage one or more of the parties to forget that this was nothing more than a business arrangement. I doubted it had been designed to protect me. Most likely, it had been intended to protect them from having me become presumptuous.

"Kaelen isn't here at the moment," he responded, a slight edge to his voice now.

Coldness swept through me as my suspicion deepened that he might be trying to trick me. Before I could think of a response, though, before he had even completely gotten the statement out of his mouth, Kaelen entered the kitchen.

His gaze settled pointedly on the two of us for several moments before it swept the disaster area Gareth had created.

I had no idea whether Kaelen had heard the comment or not, but it was immediately clear from the resentful look Gareth sent him and his faintly heightened color that I had misjudged him.

"I trust your plans for the kitchen include cleaning it when you're done in here," he finally said levelly.

His face darkening, Gareth glanced around the kitchen as if both baffled and outraged at the suggestion.

"I'll clean it," I said quickly, hoping to avert an argument between the two brothers. "He cooked."

Kaelen's gaze zeroed in on me. I wasn't entirely certain what that look meant until it dawned on me that I had spoken out of turn. As that sank in, I felt my own color fluctuate. "Sir," I added belatedly, hoping to deflect whatever censure might be forthcoming.

Something flickered in his eyes. I had the feeling he was taken aback, but it was hard to gauge his reaction when his expression was so impassive. Finally, he merely nodded and left. I stared at the door after he had departed, relieved, but wondering what had brought him to the kitchen to begin with. He reappeared after a moment, strode to the refrigerator, snatched a diet soda from it, and departed again.

Amusement flickered through me despite my anxiety as I realized that in spite of his unruffled façade he had been so disconcerted that he had forgotten what he had come in for. Sucking my bottom lip between my teeth to keep from smiling, I focused my attention on my plate.

When I glanced up at Gareth, I saw that his eyes were gleaming and his lips twitching. "He's got a father complex," Gareth said dryly. "You'd think, the way he acts, he was ten years older than me instead of only three."

He shrugged when I looked at him curiously, hoping he would continue. "He was barely fifteen when he came into his inheri ... when our father was killed," he finished smoothly. "He's been trying to father me ever since despite the fact that our uncle took us in to raise us with his kids."

Empathy for their loss made my throat close. I looked down at my plate, but my appetite had vanished. All I could think about was that they seemed to have lost their childhood when they had lost their father. I hadn't missed the slip. They had inherited responsibilities with the money, I didn't doubt, that were damned heavy for two young teens. I wondered why he hadn't mentioned their mother, but she must have died before, I decided. Otherwise they wouldn't have had to go live with their uncle.

I had the feeling it wasn't a subject I should pursue. "So … you grew up with your cousins?"

He nodded. "Chance, Dev, and Cameron."

My head jerked upright as if he had snatched it upward, my jaw going slack with stunned surprise. Apparently, Gareth misread my look of shock. "Dev's Uncle Jack's biological son. His wife took off when he brought him home." His lips curled distastefully. "Bitch. I have to say this for her, though. She stayed longer than our mother. *She* took off when I was about two."

I was still reeling over the fact that I had been romping with five very closely related men. I had thought it was pretty kinky when I had only known about Gareth and Kaelen. This information took it to a whole new level, although it dawned on me after a moment that it wasn't any more immoral to be screwing five cousins than five unrelated men and I hadn't wrestled too long with that—because I couldn't afford to be 'nice'.

The comment about his mother effectively redirected my thoughts, though, submerging me in a welter of chaotic thoughts. Sympathy was strongest and outrage as my mother's heart ached for the children abandoned by the one person any child ought to be able to depend on.

Uneasiness followed hard on the heels of both of those, though, as it occurred to me forcefully that not one of the men I was staying with had any reason at all to love or trust a woman. Was that why they had wanted a submissive? They wanted a chance to punish all women because of what had happened to them?

It seemed a little wild, even for me. The rules were strict, some even fairly harsh, but they hadn't mistreated me or shown any tendency to want to.

It was still rather deflating to think there was a possibility that they had picked me, an older woman, because of some deep rooted need to get even with a mother figure—and they knew I was a mother. I wondered a little wildly if they had singled me out because they *could* separate me from my children and wanted to prove all women were whores who would dump their kids if anybody dangled money under their nose like a carrot.

I was letting my imagination run away with me, I realized after a moment. I was the one who had answered the ad. They had had no idea of my existence until I had shown up. It couldn't possibly be premeditated in that sense.

That didn't rule out the possibility that my age had had a bearing on their decision, and it occurred to me abruptly that Kaelen was three years older than Gareth, and their mother had abandoned them when Gareth was two, which would have made Kaelen five.

My daughters were three and six.

I felt unwell.

After an uncomfortable moment, I got up and began to clean the kitchen with the mindlessness of an automaton. I was vaguely aware that Gareth was studying me with a look that was a mixture of bafflement, uneasiness, and a touch of anger. It registered in my mind, but trying to decipher the thoughts behind it only added to my confusion, making it harder to reason anything out.

He was gone, I discovered with surprise when I had finished cleaning up. Feeling vaguely relieved, I left the kitchen intending to change since I had wet the bustier I was wearing while I was cleaning.

Dev waylaid me before I could reach the stairs. Hooking an arm around my shoulders, he altered my course and headed for the parlor. Tumbling me onto the couch, he sprawled on top of me, shoved my arms above my head and rooted my breasts with his face for a moment before latching onto one nipple as if he meant to suck it off. And all the while, he was very busily arranging me and himself. Hooking one of my legs over the back of the couch and shoving the other onto the floor, he wedged his hips between my thighs, grappling with his zipper.

I was too besieged to gather my wits. I had already been stunned senseless by what I had discovered in the kitchen. I had no defense against his assault. My body, acting on autopilot, responded to the stimulus without any brain function to control it. I was already wet and panting for breath by the time he shifted and stuffed his cock into my hole. He grunted in satisfaction as his engorged flesh slipped inside of me without a great deal of effort on his part. Wedging his shoes against the arm of the couch for leverage, he began to pump into me like a pile driver, jarring me further and further up the couch until he discovered with his first mislick what he had done. Grabbing my waist, he dragged me back, clamped an arm around my waist once he had entered me again, and managed three more strokes before he came.

I was quivering on the verge of release when he slumped on top of me and panted gustily against my neck.

A feeling of misuse swept through me as a cloud of disappointment gathered over my head. I lay gulping for breath, trying to swallow against a knot of emotion in my throat that seemed as if it would choke me.

It wasn't even noon, for crying out loud, and I had already been fucked twice with absolutely no consideration for my own pleasure!

The trend of my thoughts brought me up short. I wasn't *here* for my pleasure. I was here for theirs! And I was being paid an obscene amount of money to 'endure'.

God! What had I been thinking! I hadn't even *tried* not to cum! If Dev hadn't been so focused upon getting his cookie and getting it over with, I would have screwed up for sure!

He looked a little uneasy when he finally raised up enough to look at my face. "Did I hurt you?" he asked hesitantly.

My chin wobbled in spite of all I could do. "No … sir," I managed finally.

Not surprisingly, he didn't look convinced. He got off of me. When he did, I hopped off the couch and virtually raced from the room and up the stairs, fearful that one of the others would catch me if I didn't get to my room quickly enough.

It wasn't quite eleven yet, but I decided to cheat a little. I needed a time out.

Chapter Six

I finished my first week at the mansion of ill repute by starting my period. It had been a hell of a week already. It seemed an apt ending to it.

A definite pattern had emerged, and I supposed the routine was sort of a comforting thing, because I knew pretty much what to expect. Kaelen came in to help, or watch, me bathe and dress—I decided that was because he was a perfectionist and was determined to see that one, I used good hygiene and two, I dressed exactly as he wanted me to dress. I went down for breakfast and was damned lucky if I managed to get it because someone was always laying in wait for me, usually all of them—except Kaelen. I got to 'rest' for an hour before lunch, which I suspected was more of an opportunity for me to get myself cleaned up from 'breakfast' than actually because they thought I needed rest because that didn't seem to occur to that randy lot. I was on the lunch menu. Even though Kaelen seemed to frown on foreplay at the table, most of them blithely ignored his displeasure and used the opportunity while I had my hands full to fondle me and one or another would decide to drag me onto their lap and feed me and/or have me feed them while they fondled me—because, I suppose, their hands were busy doing something else.

From luncheon to my afternoon rest period, everyone who hadn't managed to corner me and fuck my brains out, took the opportunity to do so. The time between the end of my rest period and dinner was when they got competitive, because, like the pool game, ranking was determined by who was best—mostly this was cards or pool, but a few times they went outside and tried to beat each other to death over the football. After dinner, I got my phone call to my girls, which generally depressed me, because every night I had to listen them begging me to come home and tell them again that it wouldn't be long at all before I was.

And then there was bed sports until I was exhausted, always beginning with Kaelen, and ending with Kaelen, who began to stay longer and longer, though he hadn't once spent the whole night in my bed.

This, of course, was in the spirit of fairness, because they paired off, and there were five, so Kaelen had to step into the breach.

I was forbidden to cum at any time during the day, whatever any of them did to me, and I began to suspect that this taboo was more because Kaelen worked during that time and couldn't participate than for any other reason—if the others worked, they were obviously on vacation because they rarely left the mansion. I feared that the effect on me was that I was turning into a nympho because none of the men thought there was any reason to deprive themselves only because I wasn't allowed to cum and they needed to fondle me to arouse themselves sufficiently to cum, or just wanted to. I wasn't sure which. My 'apparel' was enough by itself to make it impossible for me to get my mind off of my two main erogenous zones, my breasts and my clit. Their constant stroking and kissing and fondling throughout the day only made that *more* impossible, stoking my engines until I was ready to blow by the time the curfew was lifted. I supposed it was *also* because they had taught me how to enjoy my body and what it was capable of, but I thought it was mostly the other things.

I was sorry Gareth had enlightened me about their past. It complicated a situation that shouldn't have been complicated. I had been curious. I had wanted to know, but knowing made it impossible, I discovered, to look upon them with the distance and objectivity I had had before when they were just strangers who had hired me to entertain them.

I couldn't get that distance back, and, as hard as I tried, I also couldn't prevent it from changing the way I felt about them or behaved toward them. I tried, lord knows I did, but I couldn't, and I felt horribly guilty because both Gareth and Dev seemed to be laboring under the impression that I was mad at them and were very cool toward me because of it for days. They hadn't abstained, but I thought that was because they felt guilty somehow and didn't want the others to know, because they were very distant even when we were having sex.

I think the worse of it was that I *wanted* to smooth things over, and at the same time knew it was probably for the best if I didn't. This was a job. It would be ending in a few weeks, and I would never set eyes on any of them again. I was trying not to be stupid and grow fond of any of them. Knowing that didn't make it any easier though, or make me stop wanting to try to explain.

I felt like hell when I woke up, but then I never felt really good first thing in the morning, and every night since I had arrived at the mansion had been a rough night. My belly felt bloated and uncomfortable, but, again, I had romped half the night and since bigger than average cocks seemed to be a family trait, that wasn't surprising either. I was damp in my feminine area, also explainable.

Some sixth sense, plus a general idea that it was close to my time, told me it was none of the above, though, and when I checked, I saw it was that time. I had known I would have my period while I was away and about, but when I had considered that insurmountable obstacle before, I hadn't had a very clear idea of how things were going to be once I arrived. Now that I did, I realized it was going to be a lot more than an inconvenience to me.

No one was going to be happy about, especially Kaelen, who really disliked having any of his plans interfered with.

I was expecting a nasty scene, therefore, when Kaelen arrived.

He stopped abruptly and gave me one of his looks when he saw I was still in bed. I reddened. I really, really didn't like having to tell him, of all people, what the problem was.

"I'm … uh … indisposed," I said delicately in answer to his questioning glance.

His lips tightened. "We all feel the urge to be lazy from time to time. However, having a job is a privilege and a responsibility."

As if that pompous lecture solved the problem then and there, he headed toward the bathroom. I sat up in bed, pulling the covers over my breasts. "I'm on the rag," I said baldly, realizing nothing was going to get through to him but bluntness. And I wasn't about to get up in my condition with him in there.

He jolted to a halt and swiveled around to look at me as if I had grown two heads. I suspected that it was disbelief that I had had the audacity to inconvenience him. "What?"

I gave him a look. "My period? Menstruation? That thing that women do once a month before they get PMS?"

He reddened. I could see his mind working, turning over the possibility that I was only claiming to be indisposed to oppose him. Or maybe he thought I had just *done* it to oppose him? My ex had certainly seemed to think I did it deliberately to inconvenience him. "I can't help it," I said sullenly.

He looked discomfited. "Ah ... how many days do you think—expect this to be a problem?"

"Three or four ... maybe five, but usually not," I added when he looked appalled.

"There's no ... it's not .... You can't pin it down any better than that?" he demanded.

I narrowed my eyes at him. "No I can't pin it down any better than that. It's not ... a switch. It starts when I reach a certain point in the cycle and it ends when it's done."

He shoved his hands in his pant's pocket. "Is there anything you need?"

I looked at him in surprise. It was so sweet of him to ask! I had to wonder, though, if I asked him to run down to the store and get me some tampons if they would all be downstairs fighting over who had to go for the rest of the day. "I brought what I need."

He gave me a look. "So ... you were prepared? You didn't think to mention this?"

I glared at him. "Women's cycles are monthly! It didn't occur to me that I'd *need* to mention it."

His lips tightened, but he reddened even more. Turning abruptly, he left the room.

I settled back in the bed, fuming. Why, I wondered, hadn't it occurred to me that they might not have thought about this? *They* didn't have to worry about having one miserable week out of every frigging month! *They* didn't have to worry about bloating, cramping, seepage, and/or unexpected 'arrivals' at the worst possible time!

I knew men never gave it a thought unless it inconvenienced them. My ex hadn't. He had, in fact, accused me once of deliberately starting my period to keep from having to give him any.

It dawned on me after a few moments that Kaelen was appalled because it hadn't occurred to him at all, and if it hadn't, then he wasn't used to having a long term relationship.

He hadn't been married, and I doubted any of the others had, either. They came from a well-to-do family. There was no incentive to be in a great rush to settle down, and a lot of incentive not to.

I wondered abruptly if this little house party was some elaborate send off for one of them that was thinking about taking the plunge. It was a bachelor party on a staggering scale if that was true, but that didn't mean it couldn't be.

It also didn't mean that it was, and, even it was, it was none of my business.

I got out of bed after a few minutes and went to take a shower and brush my teeth. Dragging my suitcase out of the bottom of the armoire, I got what I needed and got my own clothes to put on.

I discovered when I got downstairs that Kaelen had made the announcement that the party was on hold. It had cleared the house. Feeling like a leaper, I went into the kitchen and fixed myself some breakfast. As I ate the solitary meal, I thought about the situation. I hadn't been bored since I had arrived because I had hardly had a moment to myself. Three or four days of having nothing to do, no one even to talk to, was going to be really, really boring.

It occurred to me that there was really no point at all in being there if I couldn't entertain, which led me, naturally enough, to thinking about the possibility of going home for a few days. By the time I had finished eating, I was excited. I tried to tamp it as I headed for Kaelen's office, because nothing had been said about me taking leave during the six weeks, but I couldn't help but be hopeful when it was patently obvious they didn't even want to be in the same house with me.

My heart nearly failed me when I reached Kaelen's sacred sanctum. The office was off limits, and no one was supposed to disturb Kaelen when he was working. Gathering my nerve, I tapped on the door anyway.

"Come!"

A little surprised that I had been admitted, I turned the doorknob and peered inside. The room was huge, but then all of the rooms in the mansion were huge. What surprised me, though, was that there nothing temporary looking about the office because I had assumed the mansion belonged to the company that had hired me. It looked neat, clean, well kept, but well used.

Kaelen was seated behind a huge desk with papers stacked all over the place. He looked up frowningly from a paper he had been studying and seemed to go catatonic when he discovered it was me.

Obviously, when he had said 'come' he had thought it was someone else at the door.

He sat back in his chair after a moment, studying me appraisingly. Lifting a hand, he flicked his fingers at me in a summoning motion. I went in and closed the door, crossing the room to stand in front of his desk.

The sense swept over me as I stopped of finding myself in the principal's office for some transgression. Not that I ever had but once, but once had been enough to make a deeply unpleasant impression on me. "You need something?" he prompted when I merely stood in front of the desk, fighting the urge to wring my hands and trying to figure out what to do with them. I finally put them behind my back.

Discovering my mouth had gone dry, I cleared my throat uncomfortably. "I was just wondering...."

His dark brows rose.

It wasn't really encouragement to continue. "I just thought ... since I'm indisposed anyway and ... not really of any use around here ... I thought, maybe, you wouldn't mind if I went home for a couple of days," I stammered.

He studied me in silence for several minutes after I had finished, making me more and more uncomfortable. "What makes you think you're of no use?" he asked coolly.

I was taken aback. "Well ... uh ... I can't ... you know."

"Can't what? Have sex? Give head? You're suggesting both ends are out of commission because you're on your period?"

I reddened. "Oh," I said lamely, feeling stupid and miserably disappointed. Nodding, I turned away, heading for the door. "I'm sorry I bothered you," I threw over my shoulder.

He got up. I could hear his long stride as he followed me. Unnerved, I moved a little faster, but he caught up to me before I got to the door. Catching my arm, he pulled me around to face him. "Did you *need* to go home for some reason?"

I dragged in a shuddering breath. Need? I didn't *need* to. The girls were fine. I knew my mother was taking good care of them. It had been a stupid idea anyway. If I went home, it would just upset me and the girls when I had to leave again. I shook my head.

He caught my chin in his hand and forced me to look up at him. "Why did you ask, then, knowing you'd be penalized?"

I stared at him. I hadn't thought about being penalized for being gone a few days, but I didn't think it would've weighed with me even if I had considered it. "I miss them," I said finally.

His dark brows drew together. "Who?"

I looked at him in surprise. Surely he had known I had children? The company had made up a file with all of my personal information. I couldn't believe Kaelen, of all people, would not have thoroughly studied the file. "My babies."

He studied my face almost curiously, but I saw suspicion in his eyes, as well. "You talk to them every night. You read and signed the terms of the agreement. Six weeks."

I swallowed audibly. "Yes," I managed to say. "You're right. I'm sorry I bothered you."

His gaze flickered over my face, and I could see the gears turning in his mind. I knew the instant he decided I was trying to run some sort of scam. It insulted me, but then he didn't know me. He had no more reason to trust me than I did to trust him.

I was still insulted and angry when he finally spoke the words I had been expecting. "You aren't really on your period, are you?"

"Yes, I really am, damn it!" I snapped. "If you want proof...."

Something flickered in his eyes. "I'm busy at the moment. You can prove it to me tonight."

I was so appalled by that threat that he had escorted me out and closed the door behind me before I could think of anything else to say. I stood outside his door for a long while. I hadn't meant *that* kind of proof! I hadn't expected to have to prove it at all!

I left after a few minutes, wandered around awhile, and finally went into the media room and flopped on the couch to stare at the TV for a while. I was still smarting over his veiled accusation, though, and worried about his 'investigation' into my supposed attempt to hoodwink him.

I'd had sex with my ex during my courses before. I supposed just about every woman had, because it inconvenienced the man in their life and sometimes they just wouldn't shut up until they got it, regardless of the state of things. The odd thing about it was, even though I had found it revolting on one level, I had been far more sensitive during that time and actually enjoyed the sex better. That had been with my husband, though, and under duress, not with a man I hardly knew!

He might not mean sex, but that didn't make me feel any better. In fact, it was worse. At least if it was sex I'd be in a dark room … dim room!

It occurred to me abruptly to wonder if the reason I had been so receptive to the guys was because I was nearing that time. I hadn't even considered that possibility before, but now that I had, I decided that was probably it. I *wasn't* turning into a nympho maniac!

What a relief!

I felt surprisingly better after that epiphany, especially when I remembered that I had read women reached their sexual peak when they were around my age.

I was still unhappy that Kaelen had dashed my hopes, even though I had *known* he would before I asked.

I was still pissed that he didn't want to take my word for it that I was on my period and any *reasonable* person would consider that out of commission!

I was still unnerved *and* embarrassed *and* pissed off over the prospect of having to prove to him that I wasn't lying.

I stewed over it for hours. When I had calmed down, though, it occurred to me that I wasn't actually being very reasonable, loathe though I was to admit it, even to myself. They had forked over a *lot* of money to get me here. I *had* known all the terms when I had signed, and I had agreed to the terms. I could whine now that I had been too ignorant about this sort of thing to really be prepared, but it didn't change the bottom line—I had agreed.

I had told myself I could handle it, handle whatever they threw at me, because I needed to do it for my babies.

As badly as I had wanted to smack Kaelen when he had mouthed that platitude about having a job being a privilege and a responsibility, he was right. I was damned lucky to have this particular job, however rough it seemed at times. There wasn't anything else out there, short of winning the lottery, that could save me. It would have been nice if that hadn't been the case, if I'd had choices, but I didn't live in a fairytale world. I lived in the real world, and it took money to live.

I was late getting to the kitchen to serve luncheon, mostly because I knew that most of the guys had decamped when they found out they wouldn't be getting any for several days, and it didn't occur to me that Kaelen would expect me to be prompt and take care of him.

He gave me a censorious look when I came in with the table settings, glancing at his watch pointedly. I just as pointedly ignored him and went back into the kitchen for the food the chef had prepared the night before—enough to feed five strapping young lads—which I had heated up.

Five plates, glasses, sets of silverware, napkins, and enough food for five men were deposited on the table. After setting the last of it on the table, I returned to the kitchen where I had left a plate for myself.

I had just planted my ass on the stool when the kitchen door opened and Kaelen entered. "Is today a holiday?" he asked pleasantly.

I stared at him, uneasily certain there was sarcasm in that polite question. "I don't think so … sir," I finally responded.

"Then I will expect the usual service," he retorted and then turned on his heel and left.

I glared daggers at the door for several moments and finally got up in a huff. I was half way across the kitchen before a light went on in my head. Looking back, I thought maybe it hadn't been a very bright light, but at the moment it seemed like the thing to do. The 'usual service' included me prancing around buck ass naked while they ogled me and fondled me. I was in no condition at the moment to do that, but I saw no reason, as Kaelen had so nastily pointed out, why both ends should be out of commission.

Stripping my shirt and bra off, I discarded them, breezed through the kitchen door and planted my ass in Kaelen's lap since I was fortunate enough to catch him just as he scooted his chair out to come in search of me again. Looping one arm around his shoulders, I studied him nose to nose for a moment and finally turned to survey the offering.

There were four chicken tenderloins and rice pilaf on his plate. Picking up one of the tenderloins with my fingers, I offered it to him.

His eyes were narrowed when I met his gaze again and glittering with a mixture of emotions I found hard to decipher, though I was fairly certain anger dominated. He took a bite of the chicken. I took a bite of the chicken and dropped the other end on his plate. "Rice?" I asked, scooping up a good sized pinch with my fingers and holding it near his lips.

I was expecting him to explode. Instead, he opened his mouth. Catching my wrist as I tried to drop the grains on his tongue, he closed his mouth over my fingers and sucked them one by one. My belly did a shimmy as I watched him sucking my fingers. By the time he had finished thoroughly sucking each one from tip to palm, I was hot and my belly was performing calisthenics.

I watched him as he reached to take a pinch of rice and lifted it to my lips. Mesmerized, I opened my mouth for him, sucking his fingers as he had mine and discovering in the process that it made me even hotter.

Several grains failed to make it into my mouth, landing on my bare boobs. He licked them off with his tongue. Goosebumps erupted all over me. My nipples instantly grew erect, and he hadn't even come near either one of them.

Slipping a hand along my cheek, he curled his fingertips against my skull and drew me closer. His gaze was focused on my lips. I stared back at him, unable to breathe, feeling my lips tingle as if I could feel his touch. He flicked his tongue out and traced my lower lip. Instinctively, I sucked my lip into my mouth, tasting him on my lip. It sent heady waves of heat through me as if I had taken a shot of hard liquor.

"It tastes better this way," he murmured, and I colored as I realized he had licked a crumb from my lips.

He slipped his hand lower, brushing his thumb lightly back and forth across my lower lip. "You know, of course, that your mouth has been driving me crazy," he murmured huskily.

Surprise flickered through me. Had I known? I didn't think I had. I did know he had wanted to kiss me on the lips, but I had figured it was because it was the one thing off-limits to him. I still thought so.

"Of all the things on that list, why not that?" he asked, lifting his gaze from my lips at last to meet my gaze.

I didn't want to tell him it was because I'd had enough sense to realize the intimacy of a kiss could make strangers lovers—it could make *me* think of him as a lover, *hurt* me. Sex wasn't the same at all. I knew that because I'd had sex twice a week with the same man for years and we hadn't even been friends. We had *been* strangers, because the day I left him I realized I hadn't known him at all.

"If you wanted that, why did you accept the list as it was?" I countered.

Something flickered in his eyes. He released me.

Shaken, I got off his lap. "Did you want anything else ...sir?"

He shook his head.

I felt weak and shaky and strangely near tears as I returned to the kitchen and retrieved my bra and shirt. The weak and shaky, I understood. The emotion clogging my throat, I didn't want to understand.

I had lost my appetite, but I forced myself to eat a little anyway.

I didn't leave the kitchen until I heard Kaelen leave the breakfast parlor.

When the sound of his tread had faded with distance, I got up, cleaned up my mess, and left the kitchen. As tempted as I was to go and hide in my room, I decided to go and hide in the media room instead—because Kaelen never went in the media room, and he visited mine regularly.

He brought me a dress to wear for dinner. I wondered where it had come from, if he had picked it out himself or called someone and had them take care of it—I figured it was probably the latter. It was a 'little black dress', skimpy, but appropriate enough for me to wear at the moment, covering enough but still sexy. I *felt* sexy once I had put it on and looked at myself in the mirror, no easy task at 'that time of the month'.

Kaelen seemed to approve, as well.

He was alone.

I was beginning to think the others had headed for the hills and wouldn't be back, but then they had only been gone for the day—all day.

It was amazing how you could get used to things you would never think you could.

And distressing how easily you could get used to those things and miss them when they weren't there anymore.

I was almost sorry I had presented myself as early as I had. Chance and Gareth generally kept some sort of conversation going. Dev and Cameron tended to be almost as reticent as Kaelen, but they were lively enough whenever Chance or Gareth were around to keep them talking.

An awkward silence fell when I had settled on the sofa, awkward to me anyway. Kaelen seemed well enough entertained by his own thoughts. I wondered if he was always like that or if it was just because I was hired help and supposed to be a submissive, which apparently meant ignored unless they wanted something. I got up after a few minutes, wandering idly around the room, looking at the furnishings, although I wasn't particularly interested in them.

Finally, I stopped in front of one of the windows. I wasn't staring out, though. I was studying Kaelen's reflection since I discovered I could without him knowing I was.

As I studied him, I found myself thinking about what Gareth had told me, wondering what it must have been like for him to discover his mother had gone away and wasn't coming back. My daughters were suffering over my absence. Nothing I could tell them appeased them or made it any less difficult for them to handle the separation. I knew it wouldn't be for long, and that I was doing what was best for them, but if I missed them, felt the pang of separation, how much worse must it be for them when they didn't really understand or have a strong concept of time? How difficult had it been for Gareth and Kaelen to accept and understand?

I hadn't wanted to think about it. I had tried hard not to, but looking at the two handsome, virile young men they had grown into, I could easily picture two adorable little boys, and it made me wonder how a mother could walk away from them and not look back.

Maybe she hadn't. Maybe she hadn't had a choice and their father just hadn't told them? Maybe his father had *made* her leave? He had obviously had money, and money could buy just about anything.

I was a prime example of that.

I pushed the thought from my mind, both thoughts. I couldn't afford to empathize with Kaelen or Gareth—or Cameron, Dev, or Chance either, for that matter. It was tragic, sad to think even money couldn't buy happiness, but that was life—*their* life, and it had nothing to do with me.

It was bad enough that I thoroughly enjoyed having sex with them. I hadn't expected to. It was actually a blessing for me that I did, because it made what I had to do more than bearable. It was a curse at the same time, because I didn't think I was going to adjust very well to my old life once I had it back.

And I already didn't want to think about never seeing them again. How bad would it be when the clock struck twelve and my magic carriage turned into a pumpkin?

I was supposed to have been detached from all this, I thought unhappily. I had been so sure it was going to be horrible and disgusting and a trial just to endure it. Instead, it had been wonderful, and I didn't think, even if I had managed to make it all the way through without ever learning anything at all about them that I would've been able to remain detached about it.

Stupid! A person could be detached about bread. Smear shit on it, and it was disgusting, jelly and it was lovely, but you couldn't be detached about either extreme. There had *never* been any chance of being detached about this. I just hadn't been smart enough to realize it. Or maybe I had just been too desperate to acknowledge it?

It didn't matter, I told myself. If it had been horrible, I would've been traumatized for life. I was lucky. I had to appreciate that. I had expected to suffer. There was no point in whining about the fact that I was going to suffer later instead of during, because this was more like heaven than hell, and I was going to feel as if I had fallen when I had to leave my Eden.

I was so deep in thought that I didn't notice when Kaelen got up and crossed the room to join me. The brush of his hand along my bare shoulder sent a jolt through me. I tensed. Feeling it, he hesitated. After a lengthy pause, he stroked his hand down along my arm and laced his fingers through mine.

I felt the brush of his other hand along my shoulders as he very carefully smoothed my hair off my back and over one shoulder. Slipping that arm around me then, he cupped one breast and pulled me back against his body as he explored the bare skin above the top of the dress with a feather light brush of his parted lips. The moist heat of his breath made my skin tighten all over my body, made every nerve ending awaken. Like microscopic radars, they mapped every point where our bodies touched and telegraphed pleasure into my brain until the sensors were smoking with overload. The light brush of his lips sent tingles through me. Heated moisture gathered low in my belly as he moved his focus upward and explored the back of my neck at the base of my skull and then the side of my neck and finally closed his mouth over my ear, sucking gently.

My knees went weak. A heated cloud of desire coiled around me as his scent caressed my nostrils, invaded my lungs with each ragged breath I took and then my blood as my frantically beating heart pumped his essence through my bloodstream.

I began to tremble with the effort to hold myself up as the strength left the outer shell of my body and focused inwardly on the building tension at my core.

I was so relieved when the servant arrived to announce dinner and broke the spell I felt like screaming. Everything inside of me *was* screaming as Kaelen moved away from me and tugged at the hand he still held. I struggled to appear unaffected, but it took focus and concentration to cross the room without wilting to the floor.

I had recovered somewhat by the time we reached the dining room, but I was still shaken, hot, and breathless.

Dinner seemed interminable. I had no idea what I ate, or how much. All I could think about was that I was alone in the house with Kaelen. Tonight it would be only Kaelen.

And damn it to hell it sucked that I was in an embarrassing condition!

Chapter Seven

It didn't help that I knew I had gotten myself into this situation. Kaelen hadn't doubted my word until I had asked him to go home. It was that that had made him question whether he could take my word or not, that that had made him believe I had lied to him.

I didn't know if it was better or worse than I had lost the edge off my embarrassment. I was still uncomfortable about being intimate with him now, but I wanted him enough that I felt more shy than put upon or embarrassed.

And that made me uneasy.

I tried to dismiss it as I left the bathroom and crossed the room naked to join him in the bed, but couldn't shake the sense that *this* was different. This wasn't like sex for hire. This was the sort of intimacy two people only shared when they were bonded together.

My reasoning was insane, of course, predicated on my long marriage—because when two people lived together all the walls came tumbling down after a while. It might seem like that to me, but I knew from his perspective it wasn't like that at all. From his view point he was simply demanding I shell out my services as agreed, determining just how much he could trust my word.

He gathered me into his arms when I had settled nervously beside him and drove all those thoughts from my mind as he strummed my body with his hands and, within moments, drew the melody from me that he had begun playing earlier, resurrected even the light notes I had scarcely been aware of for the thundering bass of my heart against my ears. The heady scent of his cologne, heated by his body, enveloped me in a dizzying cloud. Underlying that, though, was his own scent and that drove me wilder even than the cologne.

Naked now where before I had been confined by the bustier, I felt the contrast as never before of his hard muscles, silky skin, and the faint roughness of the dark hair on his chest and belly as his body surged against mine, rubbing from chest to lower belly. He entwined his legs with mine, as well, stroking his hair roughened legs along the smooth skin of my legs until it seemed there wasn't a spare inch of my skin not vividly aware of him. His arms and palms and fingers completed the circuit as he stroked them along my back and buttocks just as his legs caressed mine, and his chest and belly rubbed along my breasts and stomach, and his face stroked my face and neck.

Surrounded and enveloped by him, his touch and his scent, I lost the ability for conscious thought, lost all awareness of anything outside the fevered haze that swept over me. I wanted to crawl inside him, wanted him inside of me, wanted to be joined with him.

His breath was near as ragged as my own, but he seemed in no great rush for all that. We rolled restlessly from side to side as he shifted to caress my buttocks and back, and then my breasts and belly and then my back again. I was wet for him, aching to be filled before he had satisfied his need to touch and stroke and moved on to tasting. By the time he had skimmed my body from throat to lower belly with his lips and lathed me with his tongue, I felt as if I was burning up with the fever of need.

I opened my legs eagerly as he shifted finally to wedge his hips between mine, lifted my hips to meet his thrust as he engaged our bodies and pushed to seat his cock head within my opening. A rush of stinging sensation washed over me as he delved deeper with each stroke until he had sheathed his engorged shaft to the hilt. I groaned his name like prayer.

Gripping my buttocks, he rolled onto his back. Gasping, I folded my legs beneath me and pushed upright. Dizzy, drunk with the sensations swirling inside my head, I struggled to keep my balance and ride him as he stroked his hands along my body, massaging my breasts. He sat up after a moment, stilling my awkward movements as he hunched down to suckle my nipples, sending fire pouring through me with each drag of his mouth.

He straightened in a moment, threading his fingers through my hair and dragging open mouthed kisses along my throat and cheeks. I wanted to feel his mouth on mine so badly it was scary. Swallowing against the urge, I tilted my face away, burrowed against his neck, and sucked a love bite at the juncture of his neck and shoulder as I lifted my hips and settled again. The movements, graceless as they were, allowed his cock to stroke me deeply, where I needed him most, and I grew more and more drunken with desire at the quakes that moved outward through me like shock waves with each stroke.

"Kaelen!" I gasped on a wail of need. "I have to cum! Please!"

A shudder went through him. Uttering a sound of impatience, he tightened an arm around my buttocks, tipping me onto my back again. He slipped almost completely out of me with the movement, gathered himself, and drove into me again. My belly spasmed as he buried himself to the hilt inside of me, tightening around his cock almost painfully.

"Like that, baby, yes," he growled as he scooped my shoulders beneath one arm and levered himself upward with his other arm to watch my face as he pumped his hips to stroke me deeply. "Cum for me."

Uttering a low, animalistic groan, I let go of the thread of control I still held onto frantically and came in hard, shuddering quakes. He dropped his forehead to mine. "Anna," he breathed gustily as he thrust deeply, ground against me slowly and then shuddered, pumping his hips jerkily as his seed shot into me.

I let out a long sigh of relief as the tension left me. He lay draped limply over me, slowly growing heavier and heavier. I squirmed beneath him when he began to cut off my ability to breathe. Taking the hint, he shifted most of his weight to the bed, leaving only an arm and leg to pin me to the bed.

Thoroughly sated, I fell asleep. He roused me some time later, aroused me again to heated need and plowed into me until we both reached a surfeit of pleasure and climaxed.

I was alone in the bed when I woke up. I felt way too deliciously satisfied to want to get up. Slowly, though, reality set in, and finally I got out of bed and went into the bathroom to bathe. The bed sheets, I discovered with dismay, looked as if someone had been sacrificed on the altar the night before. Dragging them off, I carried them into the bathroom, washed the stains out, and left them in the tub while I went into the bedroom to dress.

I supposed, feeling a mixture of amusement and embarrassment, Kaelen had his proof, not that his vacating during the night was an indication of that. He made sure he didn't spend all night in my bed even if he did fall asleep.

There was no sign of him when I went downstairs, but I wasn't surprised. He was usually in his office when I came down, and I had begun to suspect he was usually in his office by daybreak.

I jolted to a halt as I entered the kitchen and discovered him at the stove. The luscious smell of frying bacon had had my stomach gnawing at itself, but I had thought it was a lingering smell from earlier.

He glanced at me as he heard my entrance. "Hungry?" he asked, returning his attention to his task.

"Very," I responded after a moment, my gaze wandering down his back to his nicely rounded buttocks. Pleased at the invitation to join him, I crossed the kitchen and watched him a moment before moving to the cabinets to gather plates and glasses for two. He didn't seem either uncomfortable or embarrassed as he settled across from me at the eating counter. In fact, he looked surprisingly relaxed.

I had to wonder, after all, if he had noticed I hadn't lied to him.

"We can go for a ride if you like," he said when we had finished and gotten up to clean the counter and put the dishes in the sink.

I glanced at him in surprise. Doubt mingled with my pleasure, but I ignored the warning. "I'd like that, thank you."

He nodded, flicking a glance over me. "You won't need to change."

I lifted my brows at that but refrained from comment. It was just as well that what I was wearing was fine. I hadn't packed a lot since I had been told I didn't need to bring anything, and what I *had* packed was all casual like the jeans and t-shirt top I was wearing.

Settling a hand along the back of my waist, he led me from the kitchen through the outer door. A covered walkway joined the kitchen to the garage out back, forming a porte couche` about midway where cars could pass beneath to reach the long, long garage. I saw when we entered that it housed a half dozen cars, all shiny new, all expensive. He led me to a dark BMW, unlocked the door, and held it while I got in.

The car still smelled new, and I wondered if it was really that new or if it was cleaned with that cleaner that was 'new' car scent. It looked pristine enough to be new.

Fastening my seatbelt as he got in on the other side and started the engine, I settled back, feeling pleasure just at being out of the house. He had a driving style, I discovered, that unnerved me just a little, but not enough to make it impossible for me to enjoy the view as the car left the exclusive area and he began to weave through the heavy traffic of the main road. I didn't ask where we were going. I didn't think he had an actual destination in mind, and I didn't particularly care.

I tensed, though, as I began to recognize landmarks and realized we were near home—my mother's home. I didn't have one anymore, hadn't since the divorce when I had been forced to beg my mother for shelter for me and my daughters. I sat up straighter as he turned down the road that passed my mother's house, hoping to catch a glimpse of the girls.

He slowed as we neared it and then turned into my mother's driveway and killed the engine. I glanced at him wide eyed, hope making me breathless. A touch of doubt flickered through me, though, when he got out and moved around the car to open my door.

Distracted by the sound of the front door opening as I unfastened my belt and climbed out, I glanced toward the sound and saw Ashley and Alexis tumble through the doorway like a couple of frisky puppies and then freeze uncertainly when they saw the strange man.

Happiness filled me, inflated me. Moving around Kaelen, I strode quickly toward the porch. Ashley, the baby, let out a high pitched, ear splitting squeal of delight and launched herself down the stairs. Chuckling, I bent down to scoop her up. Alexis had darted down right behind her, though. As they slammed into me, I lost my balance and sprawled on my butt in the yard, my arms full of giggling little girls.

I laughed with them, trying to fend them off and get up, abruptly keenly conscious of the fact that Kaelen was still behind me. I threw a glance in his direction as I struggled up and discovered he was leaning against the hood of his car, his legs crossed, his arms folded over his chest.

Ashley curled her arms around the top of my leg and buried her face in my crotch as I finally gained my feet. Reddening, I pushed her face away, untangled her arms, and hoisted her up onto my hip as Kaelen pushed away from the car and approached us.

Alexis was eyeing him with interest, but she had scooted behind me and was peering around at him. He looked down at her, frowning thoughtfully. "Ashley?" he guessed.

She giggled. "I'm Alexis."

"This one's Ashley," I murmured, smiling at him as he lifted his head to look at me. I suppose I shouldn't have been surprised that he knew their names, but I was.

Ashley promptly went into shy mode, clutching my neck frantically and burying her face against my chest. She turned her face to peer at him, smiling coyly, though.

Obviously, my daughters were as taken with his dark good looks as I was, I thought wryly.

"He's soooooo handsome," Ashley observed in a very audible whisper. "Is he a prince, mommy?"

I felt blood pulse in my cheeks as I sent Kaelen an agonized glance. He was grinning. Obviously, there was nothing wrong with his hearing. "She loves fairytales," I said uncomfortably.

My mother, who had followed the girls onto the porch, drew our attention by inviting us in. I looked at Kaelen questioningly, feeling certain he wouldn't want to be dragged into trying to entertain my mother and fend off her probing questions, but I had forgotten he had no experience with mothers, poor baby. He agreed easily, and we all went into the house.

I felt my stomach tighten as it dawned on me that he had brought me for a visit, but intended to take me back, as well. Dismissing it, I let the girls drag me to their room to see the kitty and left Kaelen to fend for himself.

He was good. I had to give him that. Within a few minutes he had sloughed my mother off and come to join us, leaning against the doorframe. I saw his gaze move around the room curiously. It was nice enough but cramped because all our worldly possessions were stuffed into the one room me and the girls shared. I tried to hide my embarrassment by focusing my attention on the girls and pretending I hadn't noticed his interest.

"I see you've got a tiger," he said after a moment.

Alexis giggled. "He's not a tiger! He's a kitten. Mommy got him for us to keep us company while she was gone."

"Ah," he responded, nodding. "I thought it was a tiger. You're certain it isn't a tiger?"

"Tigers are bigger, and they have great, big teeth. Mommy took us to see them at the zoo."

"You like the zoo?" he asked with interest.

Dread filled me. Obviously the poor man had no idea what that sort of question meant to a child.

"Can we go?" Alexis squealed, jumping up and down.

Ashley wasn't entirely sure of what the excitement was all about, but she began pingponging off the floor because Alexis was.

I sent Kaelen a helpless, pitying look. He grinned at me. "I was just about to ask you if you wanted to."

"Oh!" I exclaimed, shaking my head. "No, no. You don't want to do that!"

He gave me a look. "I believe I do."

Alexis immediately dove into her clothes drawer, searching for something suitable to wear and emptying most of the contents on the floor in spite of my efforts to pick the clothes up and stuff them back in. I sent Kaelen a harassed look and finally straightened, half pushing half pulling him from the room. "This is so sweet of you to offer," I said in distress, "but you have no idea how wild they get when they're excited. Believe me, you'll regret the invitation."

"Get them ready."

I stared after him as he turned and headed back toward the living room. Shaking my head finally at the folly of men who had no experience with children, I went back into the room and helped the girls dress.

They were so awed when I settled them in the back seat and fastened them in I didn't hear much more than a peep out of them throughout the drive. Kaelen seemed impressed with their good behavior, but I knew it was just a matter of time before they overcame their wonder and resumed their typical behavior.

Not that they were bad. They were children, though, young children, which meant they were as yet untamed little savages. When we released them from the tethers of the seatbelts upon arriving at the zoo, they showed their true colors. I had grabbed one hand of each girl, and they promptly ran in a circle around me. Kaelen caught Ashley beneath the arms before they could twist me into a pretzel and hefted her into the cradle of one arm. She went catatonic, staring at him owl eyed.

I wasn't sure if she was terrified that the strange man had picked her up, or enthralled, but at least she was quiet. Taking Alexis' hand, I held her firmly as the four of us trooped to the ticket shack and Kaelen forked up the entrance fees.

We spent the day at the zoo. It was actually not as much of an ordeal as I had expected. The chimpanzees were enjoying an orgy when we arrived at the monkey cages. Covering Alexis' eyes, I made an about face and headed toward the gorilla cage.

Kaelen laughed when Alexis complained loudly about wanting to watch the chimpanzees play piggy back. Biting my lip to keep from joining him, I sent him a censorious look and directed Alexis' attention to the big monkey.

I decided, maybe, he knew a little bit more about children than I had guessed. He was aided, of course, by the awe the girls felt toward him, but he still handled them well, except that he was perfectly willing to drag his wallet out every time they saw a sign indicating the sale of snacks and beverages. I had to call a halt to that quickly to prevent them from sugar overload.

But we walked around and around, watching the animals until both of the girls were completely exhausted. I had to carry Ashley out because she had finally nodded off. Alexis was dragging, whining, and complaining until Kaelen picked her up. "I'm a big girl," she informed him immediately. "I'm supposed to walk."

"Except this time," Kaelen responded.

She hadn't wanted to walk. Looping her arms around his neck, she clung to him, dropping her head to his shoulder.

As a plan, it couldn't have been better executed. The girls were so tired still when we got home that I was able to settle them down for a nap without much protest from either one, even though Alexis rarely took naps anymore. When I had tucked them in, I settled on the edge of the bed for a few moments, watching their angelic, sleeping faces—the only time they really looked, or behaved, like little angels.

Sighing after a moment, I leaned down to kiss them and got up to leave.

Kaelen was leaning against the doorframe watching me when I turned around, his expression unreadable. "Ready?" he asked when I had joined him.

Nodding, I glanced back at the girls again and finally followed him out.

Yielding to impulse when we reached the car and he opened the door for me, I slipped my arms around his waist and hugged him. "Thank you!"

He stiffened in surprise, and I released my hold almost as abruptly as I had grabbed him, climbing into the car quickly.

He glanced at me as he got into the driver's seat and started the car. "You're welcome."

I smiled at him at the acknowledgement, relieved that he hadn't been annoyed or embarrassed by my outburst and focused on fastening my belt. I felt like the silence between us on the trip back was more companionable. I don't know if it was or not, but I was relaxed, and tired, and I fell asleep, only rousing when the car finally stopped.

The gang, I discovered when we went inside, was back. They looked me and Kaelen both over speculatively as we came in. I was glad to see them but, still exhausted, I merely smiled at them and headed up to my room. Between the day at the zoo and the night with Kaelen, I was tired enough to tumble into my bed and actually sleep when I saw that someone had been in while we were gone and made up my bed.

I was content when I woke—more than that, happy. I lay where I was for a while, going back over the day in my mind, pleased that the girls had behaved so well. I didn't know why Kaelen had decided to give me the day with them, but I was grateful.

I shouldn't have given in to the impulse to hug him, though, I realized in dismay.

I shouldn't have *felt* the impulse to hug him.

A little dismayed at the affection imparted in that gesture, I got up and went to shower and change for dinner. In the course of that, I remembered the way the guys had looked me over as I came in and felt amusement tickle at me as I realized how glum they had looked.

As Kaelen had pointed out, though, I wasn't *completely* out of commission. When I had finished my bath, I went into the bedroom to see what I could find that might help their feelings. One of the bustiers was a must. I was in a sweat by the time I managed to wrestle into it by myself, my arms cramping from reaching behind me, but I managed it.

I glanced at the plug on the bedside table, but there was no way in hell I was going to insert that thing. One plug was enough. Moving to the table, I scooped it up and dropped it into the drawer and then went back to studying the contents of the armoire.

I found a long, flowing pair of dress pants I had thought at first was a skirt. The crotch, I wasn't surprised to discover, was open, but it still covered my lower half. It was black, and by happy circumstance, I had a pair of black panties to wear under it. The top was another matter. I finally decided, though, that the dress I had worn to dinner my first night in the mansion would work fine as a tunic. I studied my reflection in the full length mirror when I had finished and decided it was a clear enough message even for men.

Kaelen looked at me in surprise when I entered the game room where Cameron, Gareth, Chance, and Dev were half heartedly shooting balls around the pool table. His gaze was appreciative, however, when he had surveyed me from top to bottom. Gareth glanced at me and did a double take.

His reaction drew everyone else's attention, and they turned and looked me over with interest. Looking far less stepped on, they finally returned their attention to the game they were playing. By the time we had finished dining, they were in much better spirits.

Two days of blow jobs later, I felt as if my jaw was going to drop off, but the upside was that everyone else was relatively happy—not completely happy, but reasonably content to wait until I was fully operational again.

I ran afoul of Kaelen's temper my first day 'back on the job', though.

I was wrestling with the bustier I had picked out when Kaelen came into the room. He checked when he saw I was already in the process of getting dressed. His expression tightening with irritation, he crossed the room in long strides after that brief hesitation, heading toward the bathroom.

"I already bathed and … uh … douched," I announced as he reached the door, certain that was what he had intended to check on.

He halted, swiveling around to give me a look that I swiftly interpreted as displeasure. I wasn't certain if it was because I had spoken out of turn or because I had bathed without him, but I thought it was probably both. I stopped fighting with the bustier and gave him a wide eyed look I hoped looked properly repentant and then bowed my head submissively when he started toward me.

He cupped my buttocks, dragging me up against his body. Catching my chin in his hand, he tipped my head up so that I was looking him eye to eye as he delved between the cheeks of my ass and stroked a finger over my rectum. My eyes widened.

"You're not wearing the plug."

I blinked, searching my mind for an excuse. "I forgot," I lied, trying to will the blood away as I felt it filling my cheeks—the ones on my face.

His dark brows rose. "Forgot? When did you last wear it?"

My blush darkened. "I just took it out to bathe," I lied again.

"And forgot to put it back?"

I gulped, nodding as he released my chin at last. "You've grown that used to it, then? That you don't even notice?"

I had a bad feeling my lies were getting me deeper and deeper, but I couldn't bring myself to admit I had lied to begin with. I nodded.

He studied my face for a long moment. "Good," he finally said, "turn around and bend over."

Feeling more than a little shaky, I turned and presented him with my ass. He moved to the bedside table, stared at the contents for a moment, and pulled a plug from it. It wasn't the one I had been wearing, though. It wasn't even the next size up. I stared at the thing in horrified fascination as he lubed it. *Now* was the time to tell him I had lied, I thought a little wildly.

I couldn't get the words out as he parted my buttocks and stroked his finger over the bud, smoothing the excess lube on my skin. "Relax and bear down," he murmured as he breached the opening with the small tip. I tried, but I was panting for breath by the time he had it halfway in. I could feel sweat pop from my pores as the discomfort increased to the point of pain. I felt faint by the time he had pushed it fully inside of me. He stroked his hand almost soothingly over my buttocks. "Good girl."

When he left to wash his hands, I gritted my teeth and pushed myself upright. Despite all the lube he had lathed the thing with I discovered there wasn't much danger of me 'accidentally' pushing the damned thing out. I couldn't even comfortably put my legs together. It was going to be hell trying to sit with this thing stuck up my ass.

When he returned, he straightened the bustier and fixed the closure I had fastened up crookedly, then tightened the lacings and attached the restraint to the back edge. He caught my face in his hand again when he had turned me around to face him. "You look a little pale," he murmured. "Did I get the lacing too tight?"

I swallowed with an effort, struggled with a rise of temper. He knew damned well why I was pale, the ass! He knew I had been lying! I struggled with my stubbornness for a moment and finally shook my head when he released his hold on my chin.

He lifted his brows, waiting for me to admit the lie, but I merely stared back at him, trying to pretend I wasn't miserably uncomfortable.

Humor gleamed in his eyes when I remained stubbornly silent. Instead of moving away, he slipped an arm around me, pulling me against his length and reaching down to caress my bare buttocks with one hand. Delving the cleft, he stroked his fingers along it, running one finger over the end of the plug caressingly. Splaying his free hand along my cheek, he hooked his thumb beneath my chin and tipped my face up until my gaze met his once more. I saw the amusement had vanished from his eyes. "As much as I enjoy watching you with the others, seeing your face fill with ecstasy as they caress your beautiful tits and pussy, as much as I enjoy fucking your tight, hot little pussy myself, this is mine and no one else's," he murmured huskily. "I *will* claim it before we're done here." He leaned closer, placing his cheek near mine and whispering near my ear. "I want you screaming with ecstasy when I shove my dick up you and fuck you senseless baby, not pain. Don't lie to me again. And don't 'forget' to keep the plug right where it is. I want you ready for me. I want you hot when I take you. I want you to cum so hard you scream."

He lifted his head to stare into my eyes for a long moment before his gaze dropped to my mouth. He ran his thumb caressingly along my lower lip and finally released me. Stepping back, he crouched in front of me and fastened the restraints, cinching them until I bit my lip. I didn't know if they were tighter than before or if it just felt that way because I had gotten unused to them over the past several days—and then, of course, there was the mammoth plug.

He stroked my clit once he had adjusted the restraints that held my outer lips parted, exposing my tender nether lips. A jolt went through me all over when he covered it with his mouth, despite the fact that I had thought it likely he would. Apparently, it passed the taste test because he didn't merely suck at it a few moments and let go. He dug his fingers into the cleft of my ass, holding me for his mouth and worked my clit over with the feverishness of a starving man, tugging, and licking, and sucking at it until I thought I would pass out with the fire coursing through me.

Rising abruptly, he gripped my arms and walked me backwards, tumbling me onto the bed. He caught my legs and lifted them straight up, propping them against his chest as he pulled his cock from his pants, brought the thick head in line with my opening and shoved inside me. Despite the fact that I was already breathless with anticipation, my eyes widened as I felt him stretching me. I could feel tremors running through him as he stared down at our joined bodies, watching as he probed me, gathering moisture on his cock to ease his way. He was big, and it was a tight fit without the plug. With it, I wasn't sure it was going to fit at all.

My body disagreed. Already hot with want, it flooded my channel with enough moisture to help him claim me fully. I struggled to adjust to the fullness as I felt him glide deeply inside of me, fought to catch my breath as he began to stroke me with long, slow, deep thrusts that caressed the entire throat of my sex. He stood watching the glide of his cock in and out of me for many moments, his face taut, his eyes narrowed, his chest heaving as his breaths became more and more labored. Finally, catching my legs behind the knees, he spread my thighs until he could hook my knees over the crooks of his arms and leaned closer, plucking at each of my nipples in turn with his lips and then lingering to suckle each one until I began to gasp with the heat building inside of me, my hips rising restlessly to grind against him. He broke away after a moment, shuddering, panting for breath. Dropping his hands to the bed on either side of me to brace himself, he began to move again, thrusting and retreating quickly, setting a pace that very quickly had me near to fainting with the restriction of the bustier and my rising ardor.

"Kaelen?" I gasped, feeling the first warning tremor as my body gathered itself to launch.

"Yes, baby," he ground out, his voice a hoarse croak with the shudders wracking him as he reached his own peak. We came together, jerking with the hard convulsions, gasping, shaking as paroxysms of ecstasy rocked us.

He lay heavily against me for many moments afterward, struggling to catch his breath and gather the strength to move. Finally, uttering a pained grunt, he withdrew his flaccid member from me and slowly straightened, allowing my legs to slip downward at last.

I breathed my first decent breath of air when he dropped my feet to the floor and the bustier ceased to constrict my lungs so much. I couldn't seem to get my feet under me, however, to get up. Kaelen caught my hands and pulled me up when he had adjusted himself and zipped his pants.

I wilted weakly to the edge of the mattress again when he went into the bathroom to clean up, shivering with the cool air raking across my overheated skin. Too rattled even to think, I got up when he had left the bathroom and headed inside to clean myself up. He intercepted me. Dragging me against his chest briefly and nuzzling his face against my neck and then nipping at my ear lobe, he finally released me and strode from the room.

I collapsed on the seat of the toilet when I finally made it into the bathroom, my legs still too rubbery to hold me up for long.

At least, I thought wryly, he had started my day off right.

Chapter Eight

It wasn't until a good bit later that I had the chance to recall what Kaelen had said to me that morning and begin to understand that I might have been wrong about the entire scenario of the house party. I had reasoned through it beforehand and arrived at conclusions based on my own personal knowledge and experience.

I was broke. I needed money, and that had led me to think poor, which had also led me to believe that I was entertaining a houseful of randy young men who made good money but couldn't afford to have individual fantasies.

I had been married long enough to realize that men looked upon sex in a whole different way than women did, but I had still been married to a man who's idea of kinky was leaving the lights on and plugging me in the ass while I talked dirty to him—and I had to be coached on the dirty talk, because I couldn't think it up to save my life when he was pounding into me. He was also possessive to the point of it being a mental disorder.

The guys had no reason to feel possessive toward me, or territorial, of course. I had been hired to entertain all of them. Obviously, they had all agreed to it and not only expected to share but didn't particularly care because I was 'not a good woman' or I wouldn't have been for hire.

I hadn't been especially comfortable about the group sex thing, or doing it when anyone else was around, just waiting, I figured, for their turn. I would've been a lot more uncomfortable with it except for the fact that they had kept me so beleaguered I didn't really have a lot of mind left for worrying about such things.

Kaelen's comments gave the entire situation a different slant, though, one I hadn't even considered.

He had said he *liked* watching me have sex with the others.

It seemed to follow that the others did, too—except maybe Cameron, who didn't seem especially fond of it—and that was mostly why they had gotten together. Maybe it was even a competitive sort of thing for them. They

certainly seemed to enjoy competing for positions. Money
might have figured in to it. I still didn't know, and it really
didn't make that much difference to me one way or the
other. But the bottom line was, this was their kink. It wasn't
just the submissive part they were in to. They were ...
voyeurs.

I supposed, to varying degrees, most men were. If they
weren't having sex themselves, they got off on watching
someone else have sex—in porno films, at least.

I should have realized before that that was what I was
dealing with because the agreement had included being
filmed. I had been deeply suspicious of that part and
questioned it thoroughly until I was assured, in writing, that
no film could be taken of me and sold or duplicated and
passed around if I was recognizable on the film. I had
finally put that down to 'holiday memories' and checked it
off when I had made it clear I *would* sue if the pictures
were made public.

I had forgotten about it when no one had produced a
camera.

But that didn't rule out the possibility that there were
hidden cameras. I just hadn't thought about it until I
realized this wasn't a college hazing thing where all the
guys were lined up to use the only woman they could
afford. At least part of the reason they were all together was
because they were 'in' to sharing the experience.

This was seriously weird and kinky, a lot more so that I
had initially thought, and I had thought it was pretty kinky
from the beginning.

By the beginning of the third week, I had begun to feel far
more comfortable around the guys than I should have. It
wasn't really surprising, I didn't suppose, when I had been
intimate with all of them—usually twice a day—for the
better part of two weeks, but it was a change that made me
worry more and more about my future happiness. I didn't
just enjoy having sex with them, I liked them.

I liked them a lot.

And, in view of the situation, that was a very bad thing for
me to be feeling.

Even if they weren't really territorial, even if they were in
to the voyeurism, and the sharing, and the competition, I
couldn't feel like there was a chance in hell any one of

them would want anything to do with me after this was all over. They couldn't *care* about me back if I fell for any of them. I was used goods, seriously used, and worse, they knew every dick that had been shoved into me.

I *had* to get a grip. I had to distance myself, somehow. I had thought if I just withheld myself from the kissing, which was the *only* thing they had allowed me to refuse, I could keep it relatively impersonal. I could close my eyes and *pretend* they were my husband if I had to. In a dark room, a cock was a cock.

It hadn't been anything liked I had expected, though. I wasn't separated from them for any length of time. I wasn't shuttled off and tucked away in a room out of sight when not in use. We didn't just fuck. We sat down to meals together—like a family. They joked and laughed and included me in when they were teasing each other or reminiscing, or playing cards, or pool, or watching TV.

I hadn't expected to get to know them. I hadn't expected them to be 'real' to me any more than I would be 'real' to them.

My first inkling that things weren't going quite as they had anticipated either came when I arrived in the parlor for the before dinner gathering one evening and found Gareth, Cameron, and Kaelen arguing. More accurately, I supposed, Gareth and Cameron had had a few heated words with Kaelen. I hadn't heard Kaelen say anything at all, and although neither Dev nor Chance looked particularly pleased, it had been Cameron's slow drawl and Gareth's angry voice that I overheard.

"Why not?" Gareth demanded just as I reached the door. "We agreed...."

"Not now," Kaelen said tightly as he spied me in the doorway.

Gareth flicked a glance at me. "Why don't we ask her?"

I glanced from Gareth to Kaelen uneasily, wishing I had turned around the moment I heard raised voices and retreated to my room again.

Kaelen's lips tightened. "Because it's my decision." He glanced around at the others. "Anybody have a problem with that?"

Cameron sent him a hard look. "Not if you can agree that we all have some say in the decision. Majority rules." He paused a heartbeat, sent me a quick, assessing glance. "We're only saying we want more time."

Kaelen glared at him for a long moment and finally turned to look at me again. "We'll discuss it later," he said finally. "Anna finds this ... distressing."

Anna *did* find it distressing, not the least because *Anna* had a strong suspicion that *she* was the object of contention. I wasn't exactly sure of what had been going on, though. I hadn't heard enough to have any clue. Except for the remark Gareth had made about asking me, I wouldn't even have had a suspicion that the discussion had anything to do with me.

And actually, that didn't make it a foregone conclusion, I realized after I had thought about it a minute. He might have brought me into it for another reason entirely.

Gareth looked as if he wanted to continue the discussion, but after glancing at me, he strode toward the doorway, where I was still standing. Pausing beside me, he lifted a hand to stroke my cheek. His smile was slightly forced. "Don't pay us any mind, baby. Families fight."

He brushed past me then and strode down the corridor toward the door on the other end that led out onto the terrace.

I didn't especially want to go in if they were having a family argument, but I hadn't been excused, and I decided after a little thought that if they would refrain from arguing in my presence maybe that was a good thing even if I was uncomfortable. Chance and Dev either weren't quite as angry as the others, or they hid it better. When I had settled a little uneasily on the sofa, both men wandered over and sprawled on either side of me. Chance immediately launched into a discussion of sailing with Dev, which I had no interest in since they were discussing a sailing competition and I didn't know a thing about it.

Cameron and Kaelen moved to the other end of the room.

I shouldn't have tried to eavesdrop, but the fact that they moved further away to continue the discussion was enough to capture my interest. I couldn't hear much for all that, because Chance and Dev were talking across me.

"You don't think it's likely to cause *more* problems?" Kaelen asked tightly.

"We compete now. What's the difference?"

"The difference, Cam, and you damned well know it, is that now everyone knows it's only a matter of order. What you and Gareth are proposing would mean someone gets left out altogether."

"Might."

"Would. You forget, I know all of you."

"Then we do it the same way we've been doing it, except it falls to nights, not order."

"No," Kaelen said implacably.

Cameron was silent for several moments. "If we assigned five nights...."

"No. I mean it, Cam."

"Four, then, alternating, and everything else remains the same."

Kaelen let out an irritated breath. Before he could respond, though, the servant arrived to announce dinner.

I felt like strangling the servant. It was bad enough I couldn't hear very well for Chance's babbling and had to mentally decipher half of what they said, and they were determined to talk cryptically, but I hadn't even gotten to hear what Kaelen's response to the last suggestion was.

I mulled over it through dinner. Gareth arrived halfway through the second course and sat down. Apparently the walk outside had cooled his temper, but it hadn't improved his mood.

Chance and Dev had sat down on either side of me. Gareth, Cameron, and Kaelen had taken the other end of the table. I could tell Cameron had taken up the discussion again just by Kaelen's impassive expression and the dark color on Gareth's face that told me he wasn't happy with the way the discussion was going.

The battle waged on for most of the remainder of the week, but the men seemed to come, finally, to an agreement they were all relatively satisfied with.

I was burning to know what that was because it was as clear as mud to me that it had to do with me, or at least the game plan they had originally come up with. Or maybe it had something to do with their agreement?

If it had to do with me, I finally decided, I was bound to know eventually. It was the 'eventually' thing that bothered me.

On Saturday, Cameron escorted me to spend a half day with my daughters. I hadn't asked since that first time, but Gareth had taken me to visit the following weekend, and I was certain it was Kaelen who had arranged it.

I was actually relieved that Kaelen didn't take me himself. I had enjoyed the day we had spent together way too much. If he had made a habit of it …. I couldn't decide whether his reason for not repeating it was because he had endured all he could handle of 'the family outing', or because he was just too busy to go again, or if he was concerned that I might take it the wrong way. It mattered, but I told myself it didn't so long as I got to spend a little time with the girls. It made being away from them all week a lot easier to bear regardless of why he did it, or why he decided it would be best not to repeat the experience of escorting me himself.

Cameron took us out to a movie. I thought the suggestion was made, most likely, because he had heard from Kaelen and Gareth what a handful the girls were when they were turned loose in an outdoor setting. Kaelen had taken us the zoo, and Gareth had picked the marine wildlife zoo. They had behaved very well, as far as I was concerned, considering the setting and the excitement of viewing all sorts of animals, which they loved, and being treated to ice cream and cotton candy. I was doubtful they were going to sit still for a movie, though, especially Ashley.

One thing I could definitely say for the clan—they had a way with women, and they seemed to have just as powerful an effect on young females as they did the older ones. The girls were just as taken with Cameron as they had been with Gareth and Kaelen, which actually surprised me in spite of the fact that I thought Cameron was just as handsome in his own way as the brothers.

He also seemed to have a very good grasp of what children liked. The movie he chose kept both of the girls on the edge of their seat, but they were glued to the screen throughout most of the movie. Ashley did keep asking questions throughout in a loud stage whisper, but Cameron, who had taken her onto his lap when she kept bounding out of her seat, didn't seem to be the least bit disturbed by it.

Afterwards, he took us out to eat at a restaurant geared toward children, which not only had a menu to suit the 'pallet' of their age group, but also had an indoor/outdoor playground filled with other children running and climbing and squealing.

They might be seriously weird and kinky in my book, but there was no getting around the fact that the 'clan' was also a very good natured bunch, even when it came to dealing with very active, very inquisitive children. I wished their father had been even half as good with them. It seemed to me the girls were starved for male attention, but it was something they had never gotten, not even before the divorce and certainly not since. Their father was way too busy making points with his new woman's children to spare a moment for his own, which I really resented.

It had also made it patently clear to me that his only reason for dragging me into court for custody was to torment me. I still didn't understand why he wanted to. He had gotten everything, not only because he had hidden most of his assets before the break up, but also because he had had the money to hire a decent lawyer and I hadn't. And the divorce had been entirely his fault. I had filed, but it had been after he had left me and taken up with the other woman. It was almost as if the bastard had thought I would sit home meekly and wait for him to have his fun and come back and was punishing me because I had had the audacity to thwart his intentions.

That might have been egotistical thinking on my part. He hadn't shown any interest in coming back, but I couldn't think of anything else to explain why I had become the enemy he must crush when none of it, except the filing, had been my doing.

It was *completely* unreasonable. I might have been inclined to consider it the other side of love except that I had never felt like he loved me to start with. He had convinced me he did when I had married him, but thereafter I had only had the sense that I was something that belonged to him, not the sense that he cared whether I lived or died, much less felt affection.

I sensed as soon as I went down to the parlor that evening for dinner that something was in the air. I couldn't put my finger on it, but the very air seemed almost charged with excitement, and not all of it good. Kaelen was withdrawn to the point of coldness. Cameron smiled easily enough when I chanced to catch his gaze on me, but the easy, friendly way he had behaved toward me all day had vanished like mist. He wasn't as withdrawn as Kaelen, but he seemed inclined to keep his distance. Even Chance, who was ordinarily the most cheerful, outgoing member of the group, seemed subdued.

Gareth's behavior was harder to interpret than any of the others. Whenever I caught him looking at me, I was surprised to see a look that was so latent with heated, carnal hunger that goose bumps erupted all over me, and yet he made no attempt to come near me, seemed to be struggling to keep himself under a tight leash as if he was afraid to approach me for fear he would do something he shouldn't.

I began to feel uneasy, too, not just because they seemed so on edge, but because they kept their distance.

A pattern had been established long since that, when we dressed for dinner, they behaved far more as if I was a lady and a guest than their private play thing. During the day whenever they happened to run across me, even if they only passed me in the hallway, they yielded to the impulse of the moment, sometimes merely fondling me, sometimes dragging me to the nearest place of relative privacy and comfort and either demanding to be pleasured—given head—or bent me over something and fucked the living daylights out of me.

The evenings, though, had been established as 'civilized' dining and then organized orgy. Regardless, I had always sensed anticipation in them, barely leashed excitement while they played at being civilized and waited for the fun to begin.

Now, for the most part, it seemed they were determined to ignore me.

The uneasiness in me, I finally decided, was because I felt as if I had lost their attention. In all honesty, I was surprised I had kept their interest as long as I had. I was required to dress in such a manner as to go about fanning my tits and ass—and pussy at them. Even the dresses I wore to dinner revealed almost as much, though they at least paid lip service to covering me with some decency. I was only surprised that they hadn't gotten bored with looking at them before now. Then, too, they had fairly unrestricted access to the same—tits, ass, and pussy—and they had taken full advantage of it. It was no wonder they were losing interest. It was more of a wonder that they hadn't reached a surfeit of fucking before.

The realization depressed my spirits. I tried to tell myself that it was only from a business standpoint. I had been hired for six weeks, and we weren't even quite halfway through that period and they had already lost interest. Would they dump me? And if they did, would I get full pay?

I needed all of the money. All of it would give me what I needed to pay the lawyer and leave a small nest egg to hold us over until I could get the job training I needed to make a decent income. Half of it wasn't even going to cover the legal fees.

That was certainly a good part of my anxiety, probably the biggest part, but I had to face the fact that I was also distressed because I had begun to feel very attached to all of them, more for some than others.

I spent most of my time at dinner trying to convince myself that it was for the best, as long as I got paid what I needed. I couldn't afford to get emotionally involved with them anyway, had been working very hard to keep from doing so. At least now that wasn't going to be as big a problem for me as I had begun to fear it would be.

I was so focused on that as dinner ended and Gareth claimed me, escorting me up to my room that we had already arrived and he had closed the door behind us before I realized no one else was coming to the party.

I looked up at Gareth in confusion when he closed in on me and unclipped the single broach that held my 'dress' together at one shoulder, allowing it to fall to the floor. He was already breathing heavily with excitement as he traced my form with his hands, brushing his thumbs back and forth over my nipples until they stood erect and then tracing a path downward to my hips and up again to massage my breasts.

He noticed my uneasiness after a moment and lifted his head to meet my gaze. For a long moment, he held it. Finally, he swallowed thickly. "Tonight you're mine," he murmured, his voice a little hoarse.

His? A heady rush of heat went through me, but at the same time, my uneasiness increased. I moved shakily to the bed when he released me and began to pull off his own clothes.

"Pull back the covers," he said as I started to climb on top of the coverlet.

I sent him a questioning glance over my shoulder, but I pulled the covers back before I climbed in.

Unnerved as I was, I couldn't help but stare at him appreciatively as he dropped his shirt and toed his shoes off. His chest was beautiful--broad, sculpted, hard, and well-defined and so was his flat belly. Dark hair was sprinkled liberally across his hard pecs and between them. Beneath his male breasts, though, his skin was smooth except for the narrow trail of hair that arrowed downward to disappear beneath the waistband of his pants. He unbuckled his belt as I watched, unfastened his pants, and drew the zipper downward, revealing the end of the trail as he hooked his thumbs in his pants and shorts and peeled them downward. The hair on his lower belly formed a dark nest for the sleek, engorged cock that sprouted there, and that part was as beautiful as the rest of him.

He met my gaze as he straightened from removing his pants, holding it as he placed a knee on the edge of the bed and crawled toward me like a stalking cat. My heart leapt with anticipation as I watched his approach, need washing through me in a hot tide that settled low in my belly and ebbed outward so that my skin prickled with awareness even before he settled his chest against mine and began to explore my body with shaking hands.

This was bad, I thought dimly as heat rose into my mind and began to burn up reason, very bad. There was an aspect of group sex that made it far more elemental, impersonal, more animalistic and hedonistic, leaving very little room for a sense of closeness, a sense of belonging.

This was different, vastly different. I could very easily slip under the impression of being special, being important—being with my lover instead of a man who had paid for my 'affections'. I didn't want that. I couldn't *afford* that emotionally speaking. I was already far too fond of Gareth.

There was no distancing myself, though. I felt his touch and *knew* it was his touch. I felt his mouth and *knew* it was his mouth. There was no dizzy confusion, no way to focus on it strictly as a nameless, faceless fondling that merely aroused me.

It was Gareth's dark head I peered down at through heavy eyes as he bent to torment my breasts in the style that was his and his alone. The way he teased me with the edge of his teeth, bringing me to the very edge of pain and then lathed and suckled my nipples until he set me on fire, made me writhe and groan as if I was lying on a bed of hot coals. I couldn't be still. I couldn't resist the urge to thread my fingers through his cool, silky hair and stroke his head as he gave me pleasure, couldn't resist the urge to skate my hands along his broad shoulders and hard, muscular back and arms.

Gareth's heated breath and scent teased at my nostrils, invaded my lungs as I gasped and struggled to suck air into them and coiled inside of me like a seductive aphrodisiac until I had spread my legs in want, arching against his hip and thigh to encourage him to appease the ache he had evoked inside me.

He was in no hurry, despite the fact that he shook all over, that I could feel harder and harder tremors rippling through him. The more desperate I grew, the harder I fought to get my hands on his engorged cock and shove it inside of me. I couldn't reach low enough to catch hold of it with my hands. Thwarted of that, I curled my leg around his and arched against him, but that only drove me to a more impatient frenzy because all I could manage to do was rub my exposed nether lips against his rock hard erection.

I began to mutter his name beseechingly, nuzzling his face and neck, tugging at his earlobe with the edge of my teeth.

He shuddered, but he moved between my thighs at last, dragged the head of his cock back and forth along my cleft until I dug my fingernails into his shoulders in an agony of impatience and finally connected with my opening and surged inside of me. I arched upward and went rigid when he did, squeezing my eyes closed to savor the exquisite delight of feeling him stretching me, filling me almost beyond capacity.

I was so wet it took no more than three surges to seat him against my womb.

"Mmmm, Gareth," I moaned ecstatically, "you feel so good!"

He shuddered, uttering a hoarse, growling groan and seeking my mouth blindly. I turned my face away as his lips grazed the edge of mine, offering him my neck instead. He let out a ragged breath, sucked at my neck, and began to thrust slowly in and out of me.

Again, he sought my lips.

Again, I evaded him.

He moved his mouth to my ear. "A thousand dollars, baby. I'll give you a thousand extra if you'll let me kiss you."

The jolt that went through me at that wasn't pleasant. In point of fact, a wave of nausea swept through me. I pulled away to look at his face, my shock slowly becoming hurt and anger.

He swallowed thickly. "Don't look at me like that, Anna. I just want to kiss you when we make love."

I swallowed against the hard knot that had formed in my throat. "This is sex, not lovemaking," I said, my voice cold with the hurt anger that had tightened in my chest.

For a split second, his face reflected the hurt on my own. His expression hardened, though, even as he looked away from me. Burrowing his face against the bed above my shoulder, he began to thrust into me in hard, deep strokes, moving faster and faster. I had lost my 'hard on', but I didn't think it would've mattered if I hadn't. He drove into me like a pile driver, culminating within minutes with a husky groan as he came.

For several moments afterward, he lay heavily against me before he reared up to glare at me. "That was fucking," he growled. "When I give you as much pleasure as I take, it's making love."

He rolled away from me even as he spat that out at me in a hard, clipped voice. Climbing off the bed, he snatched up the pile of clothes he had left by the bed and stalked to the door. Snatching it open, he strode through it stark naked and slammed the door behind him.

I had pushed myself up on my elbows to watch his grand exit, my own anger evaporating in the face of his. In fact, shock gripped me, making my mind perfectly blank for many moments.

They had all become the next thing to obsessed about kissing me, Kaelen, Gareth, and Cameron mostly, Chance and Dev to a lesser degree. I had thought it was just a dislike of being denied anything. I thought it had become a sort of challenge to them, that they were trying to break through my resistance because they felt like it would be some sort of triumph for them.

When Gareth had given me that hurt look, I had thought it no more than another bid to get his way, playacting.

Would he have gotten so furious, though, if he hadn't really been hurt?

Or was I falling for his ploy? Was the anger just from not getting his way?

I didn't know, but I felt a sense of guilt creep over me as I stared at the door. I felt the urge to cry, not just because he had hurt my feelings, but because I thought I might have hurt his. The rev of an engine behind the house broke the spell. I don't know why I leapt from the bed and raced to look out of the window, but I did.

I couldn't see the driver of the car that tore out of the garage backwards, but I knew it must be Gareth. The car slammed into the stone wall that surrounded the backyard with a crunch of metal. It had barely stopped rocking, though, when the driver threw it into drive and shot down the driveway with a screech of burning rubber.

I raced from the room and pounded down the stairs, fully expecting to discover he had wrapped the car around one of the concrete columns that edged the porte couche`.

As I reached the ground floor, Kaelen and Cameron emerged into the main hallway, their expressions as alarmed as I was certain mine was. Some relief went through me as I heard the car shoot down the drive out front and another squeal of tires as he braked and made the turn onto the road, not much, but some. At least I knew he hadn't wrapped the car around anything … yet.

"What happened?"

I turned and stared at Kaelen, feeling guilt swamp me, feeling my nose and eyes begin to sting with imminent tears. "I wouldn't let him kiss me," I finally managed to get out, my chin wobbling so badly I could barely form the words.

Silence greeted that. Kaelen's expression went perfectly blank.

"He'll be bent on getting roaring drunk," Cameron said after a moment, breaking the silence. "I'd better go after him."

I turned to look at Cameron when he spoke, but I could barely see him for the tears swimming in my eyes. All I could think was that Gareth was going to hurt himself if he kept driving that crazy. I gulped as my eyes reached maximum capacity, and the tears gathered there overflowed and ran down my cheeks. Something about the way Cameron glanced at me as he turned and hurried down the hallway made me feel about the size of a worm.

I wasn't sure if I had imagined the condemnation because of the guilt eating me up or not, but I was afraid I hadn't imagined it. I met Kaelen's gaze for a moment, wondering if he was blaming me, too. They were all going to blame me, I realized, if Gareth got hurt, but no more than I was going to blame myself.

"He'll find him," he finally said. "He knows where Gareth usually goes."

I tried to smile at that tiny piece of reassurance but discovered I couldn't manage it. Nodding instead, I turned away and headed back up the stairs as Kaelen strode down the hall toward the garage, no doubt to join the search.

No one bothered me. The house felt empty, and I decided they had all gone out to look for Gareth. I paced the floor trying not to imagine all sorts of horrible accidents, trying to block the images of Gareth's broken, bleeding body that kept popping into my head—Gareth in handcuffs and some else's broken, bleeding body slumped in their squashed car. I walked faster whenever those images popped in my mind, as if I could outrun them.

The images alternated between the fight we had had for a while and the body in a hospital bed ... or morgue. After a while, the images that rose to torment me were of expressions I had seen flicker across his face as he watched me like a hungry cat, smiled at me, or someone else. I remembered the way he had looked at me when I had told him it was just sex more than anything else.

I wore myself out with guilt, remorse, worry, and the pacing, but I couldn't rest. Every time I heard a car, I raced to the window to look out. Finally, around two in the morning, I heard a car for the first time in hours and moved to look out. Realizing as I pulled the drapes back that the sound was coming from out front, I hurried to a window facing the street and looked out. A cab had pulled up the driveway that curved up to the door and stopped. The door opened, and Gareth fell out. Cameron, looking almost as unsteady, climbed out behind him and tried to help him to his feet. The doors on the other side opened, disgorging Kaelen, Chance, and Dev.

They were all drunk as lords, I realized when I heard them stumble inside like a herd of buffalo, talking loudly. Snickers followed each heavy thump as they knocked something over or bumped into a wall.

Having waited until they came into view to count heads and make sure all were accounted for, I was about to dash off on tiptoes before they spotted me when Gareth did. "Why, Miss Scarlet!" he exclaimed, grinning at me in a way that wasn't at all pleasant and doffing an imaginary hat. "May I say how very fetching you look tonight with those bodacious tits of yours!"

I gaped at him, feeling my belly take a freefall. I couldn't help it. He looked so damned cute with his dark hair a wild tangle and hanging in his eyes... and dangerous all at the same time, I was enthralled. The look of intent in his eyes, though, was enough to give me second thoughts, especially when he shrugged Kaelen and Cameron off and headed toward the stairs. They caught up to him, restraining him with an effort.

"It's my night," he growled, trying to throw them off even though I could see he was having trouble standing alone. "And it ain't over yet!"

Kaelen and Cameron sent me a questioning look. I stared back at them in disbelief. They didn't really expect me to take him to my bed when he was so drunk and belligerent!

Correctly interpreting my anxieties, Kaelen fixed his brother with a hard look. "You think you can behave yourself, Rhett, and treat Miss Scarlet with respect?"

Gareth sent me a look, his eyes glittering in a way that made me feel hot and cold at the same time. "Absolutely!"

The promise in his gaze sent shivers down my back, but I realized I didn't really believe he would hurt me, and I knew none of the others would allow it. All I had to do was scream like a banshee if I discovered I was wrong.

I nodded, waiting at the head of the stairs until they had helped him up them. By that time, I was fairly certain he was no threat at all. He could barely negotiate the stairs *with* help.

I offered to help when they reached the top, but Kaelen shook his head. He and Cameron walked him into my room. I followed. Reaching the bed at last, Gareth shrugged Kaelen and Cameron off and fell face first onto the mattress.

He didn't move. After staring at him doubtfully for several moments, Cameron and Kaelen exchanged a speaking glance and then turned to look at me. I saw then that neither one of them were in much better shape.

"It's ok," I said, hoping I wasn't going to regret this.

When they had left, I moved to Gareth, removed his shoes and socks, and began struggling to get him the rest of the way onto the mattress. He rolled after I had tugged and shoved at him for several moments, carrying me with him since I had hold of him and didn't let go quickly enough.

He lifted his head and looked down at me when I fell across him. A dopey grin curled his lips. "Darlin', if you wanted me naked, you should've said so."

Chapter Nine

I couldn't help but smile back at Gareth, but I shook my head. "You're in no condition to do what you want to do."

He grabbed my hand and moved it to cover the huge bulge in his pants. "That's where you're wrong, baby. I'm in just the condition to do what I want."

I refrained from pointing out that wanting to wasn't the same thing as being able to. When he sat up and began struggling with his clothes, though, I helped him pull them off. "As long as you're down there," he murmured huskily when I had dragged his pants off, "maybe you could kiss me there?"

I gave him a look. "Where?"

He flopped back against the bed. "My dick, baby. You won't kiss me anywhere else."

I stared at him as he dropped an arm across his eyes, more than a little suspicious that I was being played. Recalling how sick with worry I had been about him, though, I dismissed that. He was drunk enough it wasn't likely he was going to remember anything very clearly when he woke in the morning, and I discovered I desperately wanted to make up for hurting his feelings earlier—even though I knew I hadn't been in the wrong, that I had been well within my rights to refuse besides the fact that he had hurt my feelings first.

"Where do you want me to kiss you, baby?" I asked quietly.

He lifted the arm and looked down at me suspiciously.

"Here?" I asked, taking his cock in my hand and sucking on the head for a moment before I went down on him, closed my mouth tightly around the flesh I had sheathed and pulled upward again.

His eyes were glazed, glittering with heat when I lifted my head to look at him questioningly. I crawled a little higher. "Here?" I asked, lowering my head to suck a love bite in the center of his belly.

He sucked his breath in sharply.

I brushed my lips along his belly to the breast nearest me and sucked at his nipple. "Here?"

When I lifted my head to look up at his face again, he swooped upon me, catching me around the shoulders, rolling me onto my back on the bed, and rolling over me. He stared down at me, breathing gustily. I wasn't sure if it was the whiskey on his breath that made me dizzy, or desire. I didn't care either. I lifted upward, closing the distance between us and brushed my lips lightly across his. "Here, baby?" I whispered against his lips.

He let out a harsh exhalation and opened his mouth over mine, spearing his tongue between my lips and raking it possessively across mine. His mouth was hot and wet and tasted strongly of liquor, but it was the desperate hunger of his kiss that set me on fire. I kissed him with all the fervor he evoked inside of me, with apology, with all the affection I felt for him in that moment.

He broke the kiss after a few moments, breathing as if he had run a mile. Supping from my skin as it he wanted to taste all of me at once, he dragged open mouthed kisses across my face and neck and downward. Ravishing my breasts with his teeth and tongue and lips until I was half out of my mind with the alternating jolts of pleasure and pain that hit me whenever he was a little too enthusiastic with the teeth, he finally grabbed one of my thighs, shoved it out of the way, and wedged his hips between my legs.

Struggling for a moment, he levered his hips upward, caught his cock in his hand and guided it home, grunting in satisfaction, and he heaved upward and wedged the head firmly in the mouth of my sex.

"Baby," he muttered, contorting his body to nip at my nipples again. "I love sucking your tits. You have the sweetest nipples. I love the way they feel on my tongue."

Realizing after a moment that he couldn't suck them and fuck me at the same time, he straightened and burrowed his face against the side of my neck as he curled his hips and heaved upward, driving deeper. "Your pussy feels so good, so hot. You're so wet for me, baby."

He ground his teeth as he thrust again, uttering a groan as he sank deeply at last. "Jesus, you're so tight and hot. Jesus, baby, oh god, you feel good! You feel so good."

He covered my mouth again, managing a half a dozen awkward, stabbing thrusts, while he stroked my tongue with his. Fevered with need by now, wildly aroused by his rambling praise, I sucked his tongue. He shuddered, bucked against me, lifted his hips, and pumped wildly for several moments.

His fits and starts were driving me up the wall. I dragged my feet up and arched against him, grabbing his buttocks and trying to force him into the rhythm I needed. He broke the kiss again with a harsh gasp. "That's it baby. Take what you need. Cum for me. I want you to cum till you scream."

His deep strokes had the desired effect. I climaxed hard enough it rattled my brains. It was several moments before I realized he hadn't cum, was still pumping into me in short, deep strokes. His determined pounding against my g-spot, roused it again. The second time I came, I *did* scream as it hit me like a neutron bomb, exploding so hard I came as near to passing out as I ever had before in my life.

The quakes inside of me set him off, the muscles of my sex tightening around his cock and milking him until he was gasping and groaning and grinding his teeth. Letting out a last, harsh exhalation, he sank against me, still shuddering for several moments. I stroked his back, trying to ignore the fact that he was getting heavier and heavier.

He snored in my ear, sending a jolt through me. Biting my lip to keep from laughing, I shoved at him until he rolled off of me. He hooked his arms around me as he did so, though, dragging me with him. I struggled for a few moments to try to untangle myself from him, but I was too weak and too exhausted. Finally, I gave up and let him arrange me to his satisfaction and drifted to sleep.

The sound of the door opening woke me. Bleary eyed, I lifted my head from the hard pillow my cheek had been resting on. Seeing it was Kaelen, I dropped my head again eliciting a snore. Lifting my head again, I looked down at Gareth with a touch of surprise.

"Get up, Gareth!" Kaelen said, striding across the room and heading into the bathroom.

Gareth lifted his head, looked around the room, and rolled over me, nuzzling my breasts lazily, his eyes still glued shut, and finally found a nipple to suck on. "Gareth!"

Gareth's head popped up. Unfortunately, he didn't let go of my nipple. I winced, wide awake as it snapped back, thankfully, instead of parting company with me. After staring at Kaelen blankly for a moment, Gareth looked around groggily and finally stumbled out of bed. Scratching his balls with one hand, he scrubbed the other over his head, wandered around the room for a moment, and finally headed for the door.

Kaelen gave him look. Bending, he grabbed Gareth's clothes, wadded them into a ball, and threw them at him. "Heads up!"

Gareth turned just in time to catch them in the face. He didn't catch anything but one sock in his hands, however. When he had gathered them off the floor and straightened, he spied me on the bed and favored me with a lopsided grin. "Mornin' baby!"

I bit my lip to hide a smile. He was still drunk, poor baby! "Good morning, Gareth," I murmured as he turned to the door again and finally managed to get it open, leaving it open as he wandered down the hallway in search of his own room.

Kaelen collected what he had dropped on the way out, tossed it through the open door, and closed it.

Eying Kaelen uneasily, trying to gauge his mood, I got up and went into the bathroom, closing the door behind me. I had just cleared the toilet and flushed it when he came in behind me. Irritated that he had almost caught me on the toilet and hadn't even given me enough time to brush my teeth, I glared at the floor, deciding he didn't look like he was in the mood to take a glare from me at all well.

He jerked at the ties on the back of the bustier as I struggled to brush my teeth and then unfastened it. I gasped, swallowing a mouthful of toothpaste, as he bent me over the lavatory and snatched the plug out of my ass.

Feeling vaguely nauseated, I rinsed my mouth since I was already bent over the lavatory anyway.

Fortunately, it dawned on me even as I considered giving him a nasty look that I had been the center of an unfortunate event the night before—through *no* fault of my own! That didn't change the fact that Gareth had torn out mad enough to wreck the car before he got out of the yard and led everyone on a merry chase the night before until they had tracked him down. I wasn't sure if Kaelen was pissed about that, or hung over because he had stayed to commiserate with his brother, but I decided just to ignore Kaelen's nasty mood.

He seemed to have gotten a grip on his temper by the time he had helped me dress, but he didn't kiss my pussy awake as he had been in the habit of doing. Instead, as soon as he had fastened the restraints, he straightened and left.

Wondering if everyone was going to give me the cold shoulder, I left the room and looked around timidly. No one appeared, so I headed into the kitchen for breakfast. When I had finished, I wandered around the mansion for a while and finally settled in the media room, still with no clue as to whether or not everyone was pissed off at me. No one showed up, at all. Finally, I went back up to my room and lay down on the bed to rest for a little while before I had to serve luncheon.

Having been up for most of the night, I fell asleep. It was one o'clock when I woke up again. I stared at the clock in disbelief for several moments and finally bounded out of the bed. I could hear sounds coming from the breakfast parlor when I passed it, but I didn't see any signs of food when I got into the kitchen. Finally, I nerved myself to see what was going on and pushed the kitchen door open far enough to peer in.

There was food on the table, but no one looked terribly interested in it. Gareth was sitting in his chair with his head in his hands. Expecting to catch hell for sleeping through lunch, from Kaelen anyway, I really didn't want to go in. Unfortunately, I realized it would not help matters if I sneaked back upstairs and hid.

"I'm sorry. I fell asleep," I said when I had everyone's attention.

Dropping his hands, Gareth looked at me. Several emotions chased across his face, including embarrassment, but he sent me a crooked smile. "That's alright, baby. Come sit with me."

Kaelen scooted his chair out, caught my wrist, and yanked me down onto his lap. Kaelen and Gareth exchanged a long look. Gareth looked away first. After a moment, he muttered something under his breath and got to his feet, excusing himself.

Trying to act casual, the others got up almost as one, looked at each other uncomfortably, and finally left.

I chewed my lip, refusing to look at Kaelen, though I could feel his gaze on me.

With one finger, he nudged my chin in his direction, forcing me to look at him. "I'm sorry," I said uneasily as I met his gaze.

"About what?"

I bit my lip. I didn't really want to dredge up the incident from the night before, though. "I fell asleep."

"Because you were up most of the night."

I reddened. "I just wanted to be sure Gareth was all right," I said finally.

His lips tightened. "Gareth has a few ... self control issues," he said dryly. "It was a mistake not to send him to the military academy our father sent me to," he added thoughtfully after a few moments. "I didn't think he could handle it."

I looked at him in surprise. He had been more reticent about himself than any of the others, and they had been very careful never to mention anything specific about themselves. They talked about boyhood and college antics, mentioned people I didn't know by first name only, but they never talked about where or when anything had happened, never mentioned last names, never named specific places. I knew it was because they were protecting their true identities from me so I'd never asked.

Not that telling me he had gone to a military academy really told me anything ... except that it explained his rigid self-discipline, I thought, and supported Gareth's complaint that Kaelen suffered from a determination to father him.

He hadn't thought Gareth could handle it ... which meant it had been rough.

"You shouldn't take anything Gareth says too seriously," he said after a moment.

My gaze flew to his at that. I wondered if he was referring to the comment that had started the fight, but realized he must be. Gareth must have told them the whole thing, I realized, feeling my face color.

"... Especially when he's drunk," he added after a lengthy pause.

That comment stabbed through me like an ice pick. I looked away, trying to sooth the hurt that had caused me with the reflection that I hadn't taken him seriously at all, wondering if he just suspected what Gareth had said or if they had discussed that, too. I decided after a moment that it was probably just a suspicion because of the way Gareth had behaved. He hadn't actually said anything ... not really. He had behaved as if he was making love to me, though, and it had broken through my defenses.

Trying not to feel embarrassed that I had given too much of my own feelings away, or hurt that Kaelen had felt compelled to warn me not to take anything Gareth said to heart, I got up and went back into the kitchen.

I hadn't eaten, I thought a little absently as I rummaged around the kitchen. I didn't particularly want any of the leftovers from their luncheon. Finally, realizing I didn't actually want anything, I took an apple from the refrigerator and peeled it, ate about half before I felt like I was going to choke on it, and tossed the rest away.

Gareth was laying in wait for me when I left the kitchen at last. I braced myself. I didn't particularly want to be around him at the moment, but I didn't have a choice.

He caught me around the waist as I came even with him, glanced both ways down the hallway, and finally waltzed me into the nearest room—the breakfast parlor—which thankfully was unoccupied. I stared at his chest as he backed me into the corner and ducked down a couple of times to look at my face, evading him by turning my head. Tiring of that quickly, he caught my chin and made me look up at him.

He was frowning with a mixture of puzzlement and anger. "What's wrong?"

I swallowed with an effort, forced a smile. "Nothing."

He looked confused for a moment and then his brow cleared. "I'm sorry as hell about what I said last night, Anna. It was stupid. You're not still pissed at me, are you?"

I dragged in a shaky breath. "No. I'm not mad."

"What is it, then? Something I did after that? I was drunk, stinking drunk. Did I hurt you?"

That almost made me feel like crying. My throat felt like it was sticking together. "No. You didn't hurt me."

"I did."

I pulled myself together with an effort, struggled to act 'normal'. He hadn't meant to hurt me, I knew. Maybe he even thought he actually had a crush on me, but the things he had said and way he had behaved ... that was just ... an effort to coax me into giving him his way. I realized I hadn't really thought about how young they all were – young in terms of manhood. Men never seemed to mature like women, and I doubted very seriously that Gareth was even approaching thirty. He was three years younger than Kaelen, and I had already deduced that Kaelen, the eldest of the bunch, had to be several years younger than me.

I didn't know for certain. I didn't know a damn thing about them, really.

They knew about me, though, everything, including my full name, date of birth, and social security number—everything. There had even been a background check on me.

He probably thought I was too old to fall for his flirtation … and I knew that was all it was. I had pegged him as player the moment I set eyes on him.

I felt like telling him women never got too old to fall for handsome men and make complete fools out of themselves, but I figured he would find that out for himself eventually.

"It was something Kaelen said to you, wasn't it?" he asked tightly.

I dragged in a shuddering breath. "No. It wasn't anything he said. And you didn't hurt me. I'm just … tired. I was worried about you when you left, and I waited up to make sure you'd be ok."

He reddened, looked uncomfortable about the reminder. "I shouldn't have lost my temper with you. I'm sorry as hell about that."

I nodded. "I know. It's ok. Really."

"No, it isn't," he said, lifting a hand to stroke my cheek. "I was rough. I behaved like an ass."

I smiled faintly. "Yes, you did … but you didn't hurt me."

He chuckled ruefully.

"I'm a tough old bird," I added pointedly, wincing inwardly. I didn't, in fact, feel old at all, but the sad truth was I was probably at least six years older than Gareth and maybe even more. He was *approaching* the age of considering marriage and children and I, unfortunately, was on the down side of that slope—not entirely over the hill or beyond the possibility, but not prime meat either. Even if what Kaelen had said wasn't true, even if Gareth actually was seriously considering some sort of relationship, it wasn't one that could, or should, go anywhere. It was doomed to failure, I realized, because of my age, and also because of the unfortunate predicament I had found myself in, where I had felt that I had to sell myself to save my children—or save myself. They might do fine without me. I was going to be a broken woman if I lost *them*.

And whether Gareth realized it or not, he had already condemned me for it, already proven he thought poorly of me, or he wouldn't have tried to buy me.

He frowned. I could tell from the way his gaze flickered over my face that he suspected there was a reason I had pointed out my age. He straightened away from me. "What *did* Kaelen say to you, anyway?"

I tried to shrug off handedly. I did *not* want to say anything that might get the two of them stirred up. I was bound to come out the loser if I turned the brothers against one another. "He just reminded me that I'd be leaving in a few weeks," I said. It wasn't exactly the truth, certainly not what he had said, but he *had* reminded me that I would be leaving.

I could tell Gareth thought that was suspicious and cast around in my mind for something to distract him.

Sex seemed like the answer.

Although I didn't realize it at the time, the incident was a prime example of just how radically that one moment of weakness had altered everything between us, completely changed our perception of one another. Before, Gareth would have been all over me by now, would have instantly launched a sexual assault the moment he dragged me into the corner, scratched his itch, and gone merrily on his way. He would not have asked me so many difficult, probing questions, and I certainly wouldn't have considered, wouldn't even have thought of, dropping my role as submissive and becoming the aggressor, not even to divert him.

"Which reminded me that we don't have long," I murmured, moving close to him and stroking my hand down the front of his pants suggestively. "We should make the most of it."

He smiled faintly but caught my hand. Guiding it around his waist, he slipped his arms around me and dragged me close, covering my mouth with his before I even realized his intention. A jolt went through me that was entirely pleasurable, but anxiety shot through me, as well. I tensed, pushed at him until he released me. "Gareth!" I hissed.

His lips curled. "You don't want the others to know."

"Oh god!" I had been sure he wasn't going to remember anything clearly from the night before. Obviously, he did, much too clearly. And now he thought I hadn't kissed anyone else—which I hadn't, but I knew he was going to think—*know* that was significant.

I couldn't think of a damned think to say to 'fix' this problem. "You're not supposed to kiss me," I said finally, hoping he actually didn't remember last night as clearly as I feared he did.

He moved closer, stalking me into the corner and then bending his knees and bringing his cock up against my cleft. The roughness of his pants brushing along my exposed lips was enough to send harsh currents of sensation through me without the pressure his erection added to it. "You started this," he murmured as he dropped his head near mine, his lips near enough to my ear to send another thrill through me as his heated breath caressed my ear. "You kissed me."

I met his gaze helplessly when he lifted his head to look at me. "Don't make this harder for me, Gareth."

He frowned. Something flickered in his eyes, but I couldn't begin to guess what was going through his mind. Finally, he stepped away from me. "I'll let it go … for now."

I wasn't sure of what he meant by that, but I was relieved that he had backed off. I was still shaken by the entire episode, worried that he wouldn't let it go, worried that he would confront Kaelen, sick that I had started the whole thing just by kissing him.

That had been so incredibly stupid!

I felt, abruptly, as if everything was falling apart around me. I didn't want to hurt Gareth—if that was even possible, but I didn't want to *get* hurt either. Kaelen hadn't told me anything I didn't know already—that there was no future in me coming to feel *anything* for any one of them.

It was almost worse that I was in much the same predicament with them all. I *was* very fond of Gareth, but I was also very fond of the others.

How screwed up was that, anyway?

And it wasn't my fault.

They were all handsome, well built, young, virile, sexy—interesting, sweet, thoughtful—and they made me crazy when they fucked me.

Maybe they *had* fucked my brains out, because I was acting like an idiot.

I was *never* going to make it through this in one piece, I realized.

And what was really scary was that they had changed the damned rules on me.

I hadn't thought about it before, hadn't had the chance to think about it, but Gareth had said it was *his* night. *That,* I realized, was what the argument had been about. That was what Kaelen had been so against. They wanted a night alone with me, and, considering how seriously I had fucked up with Gareth, I knew I was in real trouble, bad trouble, if they stopped running interference for each other. I might have had a chance of making it through this relatively unscathed, emotionally speaking, if they had just kept things the way they were—where I was never alone with any one of them.

Except Kaelen—the one of all of them I was most worried about.

They seemed dead set on throwing me for a loop. I worked myself up all day worrying about which one would spend the night with me, and then discovered they had reverted to pairing off with me again.

By the following day, I had decided I must be suffering from some sort of hormonal disorder that was playing havoc with my emotions and making me nuts—or had been. I felt as if my world had been set to rights. Gareth hadn't balked at doing three way with me and Dev. He hadn't behaved at all differently than he had before, and I decided I could put any anxieties away that I had been nurturing that he would try to woo me and convince me to open wide for heartbreak. If I could just get a grip on myself, I was going to be fine.

I *was* fine. I was fond of them. I loved fucking them and being fucked by them, but that was all there was to it and when it was over … I was going to be really horny all the time because I didn't have my fuck buddies any more, but I would get over that.

I would find someone when I had the time, maybe even meet someone when I got around to taking the classes I needed. Or maybe meet someone special when I managed to get a real job. I really wanted to get back to a normal life, have a normal sex life.

I really did.

There *was* life after the mansion of ill repute. I was going to be fine.

I had almost convinced myself of that when Cameron escorted me up to my room the following night and everyone else disappeared.

I did *not* want to spend the whole night alone with Cameron, because I *did* want to, which meant he wasn't good for me.

I wasn't in a position to object, unfortunately.

And Cameron did *not* like being rushed. There would be no quick, rough tumble—maybe two—and then falling to sleep, I knew.

I was right. Cameron stripped to the bare skin, much to my consternation, and gave me a back rub. I had had no idea my backside was so sensitive. I had never had so much attention lavished on it. He had begun by planting his ass on my thighs, and sandwiching his anaconda between my butt cheeks. Despite that, he had actually massaged my back and shoulders until I was almost completely relaxed, not that I could be *completely* relaxed with that huge cock between the cheeks of my ass, but I was relaxed enough to pay full attention to what he was doing as he finished massaging my back and shoulders and worked his way down my thighs and calves.

I knew what was coming, I thought, when he got to my feet. Instead, he surprised me by massaging them, too. I don't think I had ever felt anything quite that wonderful. I could've lain for hours while he massaged my feet.

I didn't get to, of course, but I was putty in his hands when he rolled me over and started on my front. I was already so wet by the time he had finished sucking my toes it was embarrassing. It *would* have been embarrassing, anyway, if I hadn't been wreathed in such a heated, sensual fog I hardly knew where I was.

I was so ready by the time he had worked his magic along my legs and lower belly and breasts and neck that I came before he had even managed to wedge his cock fully inside the throat of my sex. Came the first time.

If it had been the only time, I would have been vastly disappointed because it was a gentle quaking that was little more than a ripple in a pond. The second was harder, the third harder than that. By the time I felt myself building toward a fourth climax, I was actually a little worried.

My mind disintegrated when it hit me. My whole body felt as if it had shattered and flown apart. The convulsions were so hard each wave that hit me dragged a keen cry from my throat that bordered the edge of a scream and drove me a little further over the precipice between consciousness and oblivion until I literally fainted for a handful of seconds.

Cameron, scoundrel that he was, took full advantage of my inability to fend him off. I returned to the world of the living with the feel of his mouth on mine, the caress of his tongue along my own, and no strength of will to protect myself from the barrage of sensations and emotion that completely overwhelmed before I had managed to gather any of my wits about me.

It seemed the most natural thing in the world when he cuddled me against him and we fell asleep entwined like a pair of vines.

I slept so deeply and dreamlessly from being so thoroughly satisfied that I only surfaced from dreamland early the following morning when Cameron breached the mouth of my sex. Already wet from his caresses, boneless with the dregs of sleep that still enveloped me, he claimed me with little of the effort it generally took, gliding deeply through the wet, relaxed channel and carrying me to culmination before my mind could catch up with my body.

The sound of a closing door penetrated my scrambled wits as I flat-lined from the third climax. I was drifting toward sleep when the sound of running water alerted me to the fact that it was the bathroom door I had heard, not the bedroom door, not a door further down the hallway. I was too exhausted to piece the puzzle together, though.

Cameron nuzzled my neck. "Time to get up, sleeping beauty."

My lips curled upward in a smile. "Mmmm, I didn't get much sleep," I disputed, yawning and stretching as he released me and rolled out of the bed.

"You'll have to catch up later," Kaelen said, not sounding the least bit amused.

My eyes popped open. I stared at him owl eyed for a moment and turned to look for Cameron. He winked at me from the door as he went out, his blue eyes gleaming with mischievous amusement.

I scrambled out of the bed and headed for the bathroom. This time I locked it before I relieved myself. There was a thump and an expletive from the other side as I flushed the toilet that baffled me for a split second before I realized Kaelen had expected the door to open and flattened himself against it when it didn't. I covered my mouth as a chuckle escaped me, trying to disguise the sound as a cough when it slipped out anyway.

"Anna!" he growled from the other side of the door just as I unlocked it and snatched it open.

I bit my lip and averted my face as I spotted the round, red mark on his forehead, fighting the urge to giggle. His thunderous expression was a clear indication he wouldn't take it in good part.

I had mastered the urge to laugh by the time I had joined Kaelen in the tub for our morning ritual. The episode had diverted my mind from Cameron, but I discovered as Kaelen bathed me that that was only a temporary situation. I shivered as Kaelen bathed me, bringing my mind right back to the night I had spent with Cameron because it took no more than a light brush along my still sensitized skin to stir up echoes of the sensations I had so recently experienced.

Tossing the washcloth aside, Kaelen got up abruptly, slammed the can of shaving cream and the razor down within my reach, and got out of the tub. I looked at him with a mixture of uneasiness and confusion, but he didn't meet my gaze. Grabbing a towel, he dried himself and went back into the bedroom.

Deciding it wouldn't be a good idea to linger too long, I shaved as quickly as I could, rinsed, and got out. Kaelen was dressed when I reached the room, staring out of the window with his back to me.

He seemed more pensive than annoyed, though, as he helped me dress.

I was relieved enough to see that he had tamped his temper to begin to wonder why he had been annoyed to start with. The only thing that occurred to me was that he wasn't happy to discover Cameron still in my bed when he had come in, but then again he hadn't said anything either to Cameron or to me about it. I had to assume he had approved the new order of things because it had become crystal clear very shortly after I had arrived that Kaelen was the grand master of all things that went on in the mansion of ill repute. I wasn't happy about the change, because it didn't take me long to figure out that the sense of well-being I had felt upon waking wasn't just because I had been thoroughly satisfied. What I had felt had gone well beyond mere physical satisfaction.

But that was a good reason for me to be unsettled, not for Kaelen.

At least, I couldn't figure any reason why Kaelen might not like it, assuming he had noticed, and I knew that there wasn't a hell of a lot Kaelen missed.

I supposed it could be because he was concerned about possible repercussions just as he had been after my night with Gareth. Cameron wasn't his younger brother, though. Cameron, I was pretty sure, was about the same age as Kaelen and not only did Cameron behave as if he felt like Kaelen's equal, Kaelen behaved toward Cameron as an equal.

I dismissed it after a while. I had other things to worry about, like the fact that I hadn't been wrong when I had suspected the game plan had been changed and the rug snatched out from under me. I had just had my defenses breached by a tactic I hadn't been expecting.

By the end of the week I was so thoroughly confused I hardly knew which end was up. They might think it was a wonderful idea to arrange more time for themselves with me, one on one, but it sure as hell wasn't good for me, not when I had already been struggling with my feelings about them. In the space of a week I had gone from fuck buddy to lover—in my mind and emotions. I couldn't speak for theirs. I entertained a good deal of doubt that it had been as emotionally taxing for them as it had been for me. For me, it changed everything.

I struggled mightily with it anyway. I tried with every fiber of my being to behave just as I had before, to merely accept their sexual overtures on a purely physical level and ignore the fact that their touch no longer *felt* impersonal and purely sexual. But I felt like a drowning woman going down for the third and last time as the days passed, and I waited with absolute dread for the one night I knew was going to finish me off, trembling in my spiked heels with both fear and anticipation of Kaelen's night.

That was going to be the coup de grace, I knew, and even while I was happy to put it off as long as I could, the anticipation was killing me slowly, making me almost wish I could have gotten it over with first instead of having to wait.

I didn't know why Kaelen allowed everyone else to go first, but it seemed significant to me and not in a good way.

He just wasn't all that interested in spending a full night with me, I realized, reminding myself that he had never even spent the rest of the night with me on those nights that he had lingered after everyone else had gone. And he had ceased to linger at all after they had settled to alternating.

Maybe, I thought, he didn't actually want to spend the night with me at all, not with just the two of us alone. He had already said he liked to watch almost as much as he liked to participate. Maybe he actually liked watching more?

Those thoughts not only left me completely unprepared for Armageddon, they effectively distracted me from the threat/promise Kaelen had made to claim the only virgin territory I still possessed for himself.

Chapter Ten

It came as a complete shock to me when it dawned on me that I had spent almost four weeks at the mansion of ill repute. I'm not sure I would have realized it on my own. It was my daughters who reminded me, not because they were any better at keeping track of the time than I was, but because my mother had reminded them that I would be coming home in a couple of weeks.

I was instantly torn. I shouldn't have been torn at all. As excited as I was to realize that I would be home with the girls in just over two weeks, though, back to the life I had left behind, I couldn't help the sinking sense of depression that accompanied that realization that that also meant in a little over two weeks I would leave my private Eden forever.

I was never going to see any of them again. I knew that. As little as I had discovered about them, I still knew we didn't travel in the same circles—wouldn't have even if I had traveled in *any* circles.

It didn't matter, of course. If we *had* belonged to the same social class and group and we chanced to run into each other, they would pretend they didn't know me, and I would have to do the same.

I was sure that would have been worse, a lot harder to bear. I was lucky it was going to be a clean break.

I didn't know why that made me feel like crying my eyes out.

I assured myself it wasn't going to be nearly as bad as I thought. The girls were going to take up every spare moment of my time once I got home, and I was going to be caught up in the battle with my ex. Once I finally got that settled, I was going to have to focus on training and job hunting.

I had everything mapped out for months. I was certain that I would hardly give the guys a thought by the time I had managed to get my life in order. It would be a distant, fond memory. I would hardly even be able to remember their names or their faces and all the time we had spent together, all the memories would just be a confused scramble in my mind, half of it completely forgotten.

God! It was going to be such a relief to have decent clothes to wear that covered all my body parts! It was going to be so nice to be able to breeze through days of doing laundry, cooking, breaking up squabbles over toys, mopping, vacuuming—job hunting--without worrying about someone dragging me off into a corner and fucking my brains out!

I was so happy I cried for hours. It was a far better way to spend my afternoon than just resting.

My eyes were so swollen when I woke up I had to lay down with a cool cloth over them for thirty minutes before I could get the swelling to go down enough to see more than a blur of light and shadows. I wasn't happy with the face that looked back at me when I went in to examine it before I took my shower to get ready for dinner. My eyes, and my nose, were still red and my lips puffy—my whole face looked puffy.

Resisting the urge to start crying again because I looked like shit, I took a long, long shower and applied enough makeup to dull the effects of the delightful afternoon I had spent by myself even if it didn't completely hide them.

Kaelen noticed, of course. I kept my face carefully averted as he helped me to dress, but I could tell by the frowning glances he kept flicking toward my face that he had noticed I had been bawling my eyes out. Wise man that he was, he didn't make any attempt to find out why.

Either that or he just wasn't that curious, I thought resentfully, immediately forgetting that only moments before I had been hoping against hope he wouldn't ask me anything because I knew it would set me off again.

I struggled to act 'normal' when everyone met in the parlor for dinner, but I was glad for once that I wasn't actually expected to participate in the conversations. There were definite advantages to being a submissive. I wasn't required to have any social graces.

I was just the dress up doll they set in the corner to ogle to get their juices flowing and fondle and fuck when they were aroused enough to look around for a vessel.

They were real people. *I* wasn't. I wasn't supposed to have any feelings one way or the other.

The servant appeared to announce dinner before I could get myself *really* worked up into seething resentment. He might as well have put grass on my plate. I had no idea what I ate, but I did begin to suspect that I had imbibed a little too much wine when I lifted my head to look down the table and give Kaelen the evil eye and discovered I had to hold on to the edges of the table to keep from falling out of my chair.

Cameron took my wine glass and put water in front of me.

He was always watching out for me.

The ass hole!

The up side to eating almost nothing and drinking far too much was that I was convinced when Kaelen helped me up from my chair and walked me upstairs that he was taking me to my room to sleep it off. As soon as he opened the door, I pulled my arm from his grasp, wobbled over to the bed and fell in face first.

He pulled my heels off and rolled the stockings down my legs, dropping them to the floor beside my shoes.

"Thank you, Kael," I muttered. "Good night."

He dragged me out of the bed. Bracing myself with an effort when he stood me upright, I stared up at him in confusion as he pulled my dress off, widening my eyes to try to keep them focused on his face. It dawned on me after a moment that he wasn't looking particularly pleased with me. "Did I do something wrong ... again?" I asked warily as he caught my shoulders and turned me so that my back was to him.

"I'll let you think about that," he said tightly as he loosened the lacing and then unfastened the hooks along the back of the bustier. "And while you're at it," he added next to my ear, "think about why I might feel like paddling your ass."

I thought he was going to when he shoved me face down on the bed. Instead, he removed the plug from my ass. Relief flooded me. Thank god he had taken that damned thing out! I could sleep a *lot* better without it!

"You're mad at me *all* the time," I informed him when he yanked me up again. "And I hardly ever know why," I added, my chin wobbling faintly as I dwelt on the sense of misusage I felt over that.

He caught my chin. "If you start that again, I *will* paddle your ass," he growled, effectively diverting me from the urge to cry.

"I think that's SBDM not submission," I informed him when I had given it some thought.

His lips twitched at the corners. "BDSM, you silly twit."

"That's what I said."

"This may come as a shock to you, dear heart, but I don't know or care what any of it's called. I know what I like, and I know what I want. The only thing that matters to me is that *you* are willing to give me anything I want."

I smiled up at his face as he slipped an arm behind my back and one beneath my knees and lifted me against his chest. "I am," I assured him just as he tossed me onto the mattress. I hit the bed with a bounce and threw my arms and legs out to keep from rolling off as the world spun around me. Kaelen grounded me when he had climbed into the bed by planting his chest on mine. I wrapped my arms around his neck. "Don't be mad at me, Kael," I said cajolingly. "I'm sorry about whatever I did."

He levered himself onto his elbows to look at me, much to my relief because he had been crushing my lungs. His gaze flickered over my face. "The question most dominate in my mind at the moment is how much you're going to remember tomorrow," he murmured finally, shifting upward until his face was directly above mine. His gaze moved to my mouth as he said it. He let out a gusty breath of impatience. "Fuck it," he growled, "sue me."

My jaw slackened in surprise. My lips parted as I sucked in a breath to ask him what he was talking about. I didn't get the chance to get anything said, though. His mouth was hot as his lips covered mine, so wildly intoxicating that I instantly lost my train of thought as his tongue raked boldly, possessively across mine, stroked it, entwined with it. I uttered a sound of surrender in my throat as I tightened my arms around his neck and kissed him back with all the longing I had bottled up inside of me for weeks. I realized I had fantasized about the way his mouth would feel on mine from the first moment I had seen it, felt my belly tremble with excitement just looking at it.

It surpassed my wildest imaginings. His touch, the taste of him on my tongue, made we so drunk with pleasure that I was reeling by the time he broke the kiss and explored the rest of my face with his lips. Panting for breath, I nuzzled him dizzily as he explored my face and came back to my mouth, traced shivery kisses along my throat and neck, and retuned to my mouth.

I wanted to feel his mouth all over me, *knew* how good his kisses felt everywhere he caressed me with it, and yet I was reluctant to give up the taste and feel of him on my mouth.

His forays thrilled me to my core, and yet I was desperate with longing again each time he returned to my mouth to give me a brief taste of the feel of his. Grateful to the depths of my soul, I stroked his head as he finessed my nipples one at the time until I was on fire with need, struggling to caress whatever part of his body I could reach with my hands when I had to accept that I couldn't reach him to kiss him back.

We surged restlessly together, arms and legs entangling, stroking body to body, leg to leg, rolling around like wrestlers as each of us struggled to achieve maximum contact and at the same time tried to reach those parts we most wanted to caress. He roamed beyond my reach finally. A shiver skated over me as I felt the loss of his heat, but the flick of his tongue on my clit sent a fresh wave of fire through me, enveloping me in a cloud of warmth.

I tangled my fingers in his hair as he continued to tug at me until I felt myself shuddering on the verge of climax. "Kael!" I gasped desperately, groaning as another wave hit me and I could feel my insides quivering. "I'm going to cum if you don't stop!"

He disentangled my tugging fingers, manacled them on the bed on either side of my hips, and continued the assault on my senses while I fought and writhed and begged.

I felt as if I was going to die if I didn't come, and yet I was frantic to have him inside of me when I did. I was nearly weeping for him when at last he stopped and surged over me, impaling me on his shaft almost in the same motion. My breath left me in a grunt as the head of his cock rammed against the mouth of my sex, breached it, slipped deeper as he cupped his hips toward mine and drove upward. We clutched at each other, heaving together with a frantic, mindless desperation to join our bodies that slickened both of us with perspiration and brought us both to culmination within moments of at last achieving union.

Kaelen found my mouth blindly as the shock waves broke over both of us almost simultaneously. I groaned, sucking at his tongue even as he sucked at mine in a gusty tangle of mouths and tongues.

Replete, we sank together toward oblivion, drowsing lazily, shifting after a few moments to a more comfortable position but remaining entangled with one another, our chests brushing with each gasp we took trying to catch our breaths. He stroked me lazily from time to time, tightened his arms around me, nuzzled his face against me and then searched for my lips, sometimes sealing his briefly with mine, sometimes merely brushing his lips along mine.

After a time, when we had cooled, caught our breaths, his caresses became more purposeful, aroused rather than soothed. Lethargic and thoroughly sated, I responded sluggishly at first, but he coaxed a budding of warmth from me with his lips and hands.

With patient determination, he stroked and kissed me until the warmth blossomed into heat and the heat into fire that demanded assuagement.

He shifted to support himself on one elbow, skimming a hand down my belly and then traced my cleft until he reached the bud below my sex. I opened my eyes and looked up at him dizzily as I felt his finger lightly stroking me there. "I want you here," he said huskily.

I felt my throat close with sudden doubt, but I had told him I was willing to give him whatever he wanted, and I was. I nodded. He moved away from me to get the lubricant from the drawer beside the bed, and I rolled over, getting to my knees shakily.

He caught me around the waist when he returned, rolling me onto my back. "This way," he said huskily. "I want to watch your face."

Confused but willing, I drew my knees up as he positioned himself between my thighs. I gasped as he began to slowly penetrate me.

"Relax, baby," he murmured raggedly. "Push for me."

I was too disoriented to make sense of the directions. It was more instinct that guided me, or maybe familiarity because of the times he had penetrated me with the plug before. I dragged in a shuddering breath and panted as he breached my opening and moved deeper, feeling a moment of panic as I realized this was nothing like the plug.

He paused, stroking me with shallow thrusts as he shifted onto one arm and reached to knead my breasts with his hands. The panic left me as I grew accustomed to the feel of him inside me. He thrust deeper as he slipped one hand down my belly and began to stroke my clit. The heat rose in me again as he strummed that nub, and I began lifting my hips to meet his strokes.

Releasing a harsh breath, he began to move faster. I felt quivers of pleasurable sensation inside of me as he did. The sensation built, grew harder, stronger until I was gasping and groaning again with imminent release. He shuddered all over when I came, bucking against him a little frantically as I was caught up in the throes of release.

As I hit my crescendo, he began to pump into me at a frantic pace until at last, with a choked cry, he stopped, and I felt his cock jerking as it expelled his hot seed inside of me.

Quivering with weakness, I went perfectly limp. He gathered himself, pushing upwards and climbing off of me. The bed dipped as he got off of it. Dimly, I heard the splash of water in the bathroom and then the bed dipped again. He was still breathing gustily as he settled beside me and dragged me into his arms. I snuggled my face against his chest, delighting in the feel of him against my face, his scent enveloping me in a cocoon of bliss, sated with my own pleasure and even more pleased about the fact that he had claimed me at last and it had felt fabulous.

* * * *

I frowned when the silly jingle on my cell phone woke me, rolled onto my belly, and pulled a pillow over my head. Kaelen had left near daylight, but I had hardly slept a wink between the time we had come up to my room and then, and when he had left I had simply rolled over and gone back sleep.

The melody stopped after a few moments. I had just let out a sigh of relief when it started again, demanding I answer.

Pushing myself upright, I crawled to edge of the bed and managed to get the phone out of the drawer before it stopped again. I stared at it blearily, trying to focus my eyes enough to read the number that had called. Before I had managed to get it into focus, the phone rang again.

I depressed the button and put it to my ear. "Hello?"

"Annabelle! For god's sake I've been calling and calling!"

I bolted upright at the sound of my mother's voice, my heart jumpstarted into an all out gallop. "What is it?" I demanded hoarsely.

"He *took* them!"

"Who?"

"William--the bastard!" my mother wailed. "They were playing in the backyard! I had just checked on them, and then I heard a car door slam and when I went outside, he was tearing out of the driveway!"

Shock closed over me. "William? What was he doing there?" I finally managed, feeling sick to my stomach.

"He took the girls!" my mother practically screamed at me. "I called the police, but they're saying they can't do anything."

"Oh god! Oh my god! I'm coming!" I said, throwing the phone down and practically falling out of the bed. "I'm coming!" I ran around in circles for a few moments, trying to think what to do and finally dove into the armoire for my clothes. I didn't bother to put on anything more than outer wear, stuffed my feet into my tennis shoes and then dashed out of the door before I remembered my purse had my car keys in it. Whirling, I ran back in to get my suitcase. I was halfway out the door the second time before I remembered my purse wasn't in it.

Uttering a sob, I ran back inside, looked wildly around, and finally remembered I had left my purse in the bathroom.

I almost fell down the stairs in my rush to get down.

Kaelen caught me before I could get to the door. Curling a hand around my upper arm, he swung me around to face him. "What are you doing?"

I stared at him blankly, still trying to wrap my mind around my disaster. "I have to go."

His face went blank and then taut with anger. "Leave? You're just going to walk out?"

"Yes," I said, tugging to free my arm from his grip. "I have to leave."

"You breach contract, you forfeit the money," he ground out.

"For god's sake, Kael!" Gareth growled.

I glanced at Gareth, saw Cameron beside him, and then discovered the commotion had drawn all of them. "It doesn't matter. It doesn't matter anymore. He took them."

Kaelen caught both my shoulders and shook me. "What are you talking about?"

"I don't need the money now," I wailed. "I only did it for them, and they're gone! He took them. I have to go. I have to try to get them back."

Abruptly Kaelen dragged me tightly against his chest, holding me in spite of my struggles to free myself. "Gareth! Get Carl Johnston on the phone. Tell him to find out where that son-of-a-bitch William Patrick is. Tell him to call me on my cell when he's tracked him down," he roared furiously.

Kaelen loosened his hold on me, but he didn't let go. Prying my suitcase out of my hand, he handed it to Cameron, then caught my arm and began to drag me down the hallway. I fought to get loose, my rubber soled shoes squeaking on the marble tile, until I realized finally that he was heading toward the garage. I tried to race him to the car then, but he held onto me, holding me back.

"This isn't helping anything, Anna," he said finally, dragging me to a halt when we reached the car. "Try to calm down, baby. We'll get them back."

I stared at him for a moment and lost it, bursting into tears. "I want my babies!" I wailed.

Kaelen wrapped his arms around me, holding me tightly, cradling my head against his chest as sobs tore from me. I knew he was trying to help. I knew he was trying to calm me down, and I needed to think, but I couldn't seem to stop once I started. He held me until I wore myself out and finally helped me into the car and fastened my seatbelt for me.

I searched my purse for a tissue to blow my nose and dry my eyes as he moved around the car to the driver's side and finally found a napkin from a fast food restaurant. The logo on the napkin nearly set me off again. It was from the restaurant Cameron had taken me and the girls to.

A police car was parked in front of my mother's house when we arrived. I unbuckled my belt and jumped out before Kaelen could come around to help me, racing across the yard to where my mother was talking to the policeman.

"Is this the mother?" the man asked with calm disinterest.

I wanted to slap him. How dare he act like it was nothing! "Yes!" I answered quickly. "You'll go get them back?"

He pursed his lips, flicked a look at Kaelen as if he was expecting one of those commiserating male looks. I glared at Kaelen, daring him to agree with the man that, yes, I was a hysterical female and just needed to be patted on the head. Kaelen's face was taut, his lips a thin line.

The cop stared at him for a long, long moment and finally looked away. "Ma'am, all we can do is go and talk to him. This is a custody situation."

"I *have* custody!"

"Your mother said there was a court hearing coming up."

I glared at my mother. "I've still got custody now."

He shook his head. "Ma'am, I hate to tell you this but possession is nine tenths of the law. He's their father. We can't legally remove them from his house. It isn't kidnapping as long as there's an open custody dispute."

I had to fight the urge to punch the man in the nose. "Then I'll go...."

Kaelen clamped a hand over my mouth. "Shut up, Anna, and go in the house. I mean it."

I glared at him over the top of his hand, but I realized abruptly that he was trying to keep me from getting arrested. I wouldn't have cared if it would get my children back, but it wouldn't. Worse, it wouldn't look good to have an arrest record when I got to court. Jerking away from him abruptly, I ran into the house.

"Women," the cop muttered. "Say ... aren't you...."

I slammed the door behind me before I heard anything else. I didn't actually register what the cop had said.

"I knew the cops would be useless," my mother said, having followed me into the house and flopped into her favorite chair. "I'm so sorry, Anna! I never thought that bastard would have the nerve to come right up in the yard! In broad daylight!"

I bit my lip to keep from saying something I would regret, pacing the floor restlessly while I tried to think. "You'd think we could at least get him for trespassing!"

Kaelen came in, closing the door behind him. "You could, but that wouldn't get the girls."

I stared at him forlornly a moment and finally wilted onto the couch, covering my face with my hands. Guilt consumed me. If I had been here, I thought, it wouldn't have happened. William might have been stupid enough to try it, but I would have fought him ... and then I probably would have gone to jail for assaulting him. I knew there was no point in blaming my mother. How could she have guessed he would pull such a stunt? The girls couldn't be kept inside all the time.

And I still blamed her, and I blamed me, and I hated William worse than I had when I had divorced him.

Kaelen settled beside me, rubbing my back for several moments, and finally tugged my hands away from my face and pulled me into his arms. "I'll get them back for you, baby," he murmured soothingly. "I swear it."

I wanted to believe him. I slipped my arms around his waist, clinging to him, clinging to the hope that he could do what he promised.

When his phone rang, he shifted me in his arms and pulled it from his pocket. "Yes?"

I pulled away, watching his face for something that would give me hope. He smiled grimly after a moment and sent me a look. "Keep watch and make sure he stays put." He listened a moment longer. "Figure it out and let me know what the plan is when you come up with something."

I looked at him hopefully when he hung up.

"Johnston found them ... no real effort. He took them and went to his place."

I dimly remembered him saying something about a man named Johnston, but I wasn't sure who he was or how the man knew where William's house was. *I* didn't even know. He had sold the house we had shared during our marriage—according to him to pay off debts we both owed, but then he had turned around and bought a new house for his new wife.

"What do we do now?"

"Wait. He'll call us when he's figured out how to get them out."

I wanted to go straight over to William's house, shoot him in the head, and take my daughters. Fortunately, I didn't have a gun or access to one. And then, too, I didn't know how to use one.

And I couldn't shoot him in front of the girls, even if I wanted to.

Kaelen could take him, though.

But I didn't want Kaelen to end up in jail.

Exhausted, I finally dozed off with my head on Kaelen's shoulder. He roused me, helped me to my feet, and walked me to the bedroom I had shared with my daughters. I felt like crying when I saw their toys scattered around the room and all over the bed. Rescuing Ashley's favorite doll as Kaelen swept the toys from the bed and told me to lie down, I cuddled it against my chest and lay down. He sat beside me, stroking a hand soothingly along my back until I fell asleep.

When Kaelen shook me awake, I discovered the room was dark. Memory flooded back quickly, though, and I sat up, looking up at him expectantly.

"Johnston called. We need to go."

I had fallen asleep fully clothed, but Kaelen—I thought—had pulled my shoes off. The overhead light blinded me for a moment when he flipped it on, but I found my shoes and slipped them onto my feet again.

There was no sign of my mother. "Mom?"

"I sent her ahead of us. She'll meet us there."

Nodding, although I didn't have a clue of where 'there' was, I locked up behind myself and followed him out to the car. The drive was a fairly short one, and I was still keyed up by the time Kaelen pulled up to the edge of the street and parked the car. The man that stepped out of the darkness as we walked quickly along the sidewalk scared the shit out of me.

"They're sleeping like babies."

I glanced at the man sharply. "The girls?" I asked quietly, using the same quiet tone he had used.

"Patrick and his woman."

Confused, I glanced at Kaelen.

"Likely to wake up?" Kaelen asked.

"Not before morning ... not if an airplane landed on the house," the man responded with satisfaction.

Kaelen's hand tightened on my arm. "We'd better move fast anyway. I don't want to be caught inside by a nosey neighbor."

We paused at the front door of a house, and the man Kaelen had called Johnston opened the door and walked right in. "The girls are in the back bedroom."

He led us to it, opening the door silently.

I shoved my way between the two men and rushed inside. Ashley and Alexis were curled up together on a small bed against one wall. Profound relief washed over me as I hurried to them and bent down to take Ashley in my arms. She complained but snuggled against my shoulder when I shushed her. Kaelen scooped Alexis up and turned to look at me.

Letting out a deep sigh, I headed out again, hurrying, fearful that William might wake up regardless of what the man had said. I had to rouse the girls to get their seatbelts on. Alexis stared at us blankly for several moments and finally smiled. "Mommy!"

I wanted to crawl into the backseat and cuddle both them just to assure myself I really had them, but I was too uneasy about the possibility Kaelen had mentioned, fearful that if we didn't leave quickly the police would show up. Stroking her head, I kissed her and told her to go back to sleep.

I didn't know where Kaelen was taking us, and I didn't care as long as it was someplace where William wouldn't find us. I stared out the window as he drove, mentally counting the money in my pocketbook and checking account. It didn't take long to count. I thought if we stayed at a really, really cheap hotel, I might have enough for two or three nights.

I should be able to access the money in the account the company had set up for me, though. I had reneged on the last couple of weeks, and that was going to be cutting things close, but I decided there was enough to rent a place for a month ... if I could find someone willing to let a place for that short a time.

I wasn't going to take them back to my mother's house, not until I had settled things in court.

A couple of hours later, Kaelen slowed the car, dragging me from my thoughts. I watched as he turned into a gated driveway. A man stepped from a security booth. "Mr. Westmoreland! Good evening!"

He stepped back inside, and the iron gates began to slowly open.

I stared at them blankly, though, too shocked to think, feeling first fiery hot and then ice cold. I didn't look at Kaelen. I felt weak all over and so nauseated I thought for several panicked moments that I was going to throw up … in Kaelen Westmoreland's car.

The Westmorelands were a private bunch, very eccentric most people said, carefully avoiding publicity of any kind because they liked their privacy, guarded it ferociously, but it would have been hard to find anyone who didn't know who they were … because the Westmorelands were one of the wealthiest families in the world.

Chapter Eleven

I felt weak all over when Kaelen helped me from the car, so weak I could hardly stand. I braced myself as I pulled Ashley from the car, uncomfortable about Kaelen carrying Alexis in, although I didn't see an alternative. I damned sure wasn't going to leave her in the car out front, and I couldn't carry both of them.

I didn't even know why we were here, but I was too numb with shock to think about asking. I just followed Kaelen.

The mansion of ill repute that I had been staying in for weeks must have been a 'get away retreat' because it could have been set down, I was pretty sure, in the grand foyer. A sweeping curved stair spiraled up from it, each side every bit of six feet wide. I glanced up and reeled dizzily as I glimpsed a dome high above the foyer. Focusing carefully on the steps after that, I shifted Ashley in my arms as she roused sleepily and then looked around the place owl eyed.

"Mommy, where's this?" she whispered as I clutched her tightly with one arm and the banister with the other. Her voice echoed eerily, and her eyes widened with delight.

"Not a peep," I hissed at her, knowing instantly that she would be shouting just to hear her voice echo.

Kaelen glanced back at me as he reached the second floor landing. Alexis, I saw, was awake, too, staring around her with a mixture of fear and awe. Kaelen set her on her feet and took her hand, leading her down the broad upper hall that looked big enough to land a 747 in it. I hurried to catch up and take her other hand when she looked back at me with wide frightened eyes.

"Where's daddy?"

"At his house," I answered her shortly. "I didn't want to wake you up when I came to get you so we just carried you to the car."

Kaelen sent me a glance but evaded his gaze.

We arrived finally at a set of double doors. Depressing one of the lever handles, Kaelen pushed the door open and stepped back for us to go in.

Alexis and Ashley both gasped with awed delight.

I felt pretty much the same emotion wash over me like a tidal wave.

It was a playroom filled with everything imaginable.

On the far side, a woman who looked to be around my age was sitting with a dark haired boy who looked about Ashley's age. The little boy's face brightened as we came in. "Daddy!" he squealed racing across the room and launching himself at Kaelen.

I covered my mouth with my hand. "Is there a bathroom …?" I asked a little desperately.

The woman took one look at my face and jumped from the rocking chair, moving quickly toward a door at the other end. I dashed toward it, sweating with the fear that I wasn't going to make it. Ashley and Alexis, babbling excitedly, were right on my heels, trying to race me to the door. and I nearly fell over them. I managed to lock the door behind us and dashed for the toilet. I didn't actually make it, but I was close.

Ashley and Alexis stood on either side of me while I barfed, their fingers in their ears to block out the gagging noise, keeping a running commentary going while I emptied my stomach.

"Eew, yuck!"

"Are you sick, Mommy?"

"That smells!"

"She ate something that didn't agree with her tummy, didn't you, Mommy?"

I leaned my head weakly against my arm when my stomach finally stopped heaving. "Please, girls!" I moaned.

Ashley patted my back. "Poor mommy."

Alexis went to get a bath cloth for me. She came back and handed it to me, dripping with water. I was grateful to have it anyway. When I had rung out the excess water, I mopped my face with it.

There was a tap on the door. "Anna?"

Before I could stop the little snots, they raced each other to the door and snatched it open.

"Don't come in!" I yelled.

Thankfully, he didn't. "Are you all right?" he asked from the doorway.

"Mommy barfed," Alexis announced.

As if she needed to! "I'll be ok in a minute!" I muttered.

"Why don't you girls come out here and meet Kael?"

When everybody had finally left, I mopped up the mess I had made with toilet paper and flushed the toilet. Feeling too weak to worry about finding cleanser to finish the job at the moment, I crawled over to the wall and sat with my back against it, my head in my hands.

He wasn't just rich. He was married. I felt a little hysterical, more than a little hysterical, actually. As if it *mattered* whether or not he was married! That was his problem, not mine! He was the one in the wrong. I hadn't made any vows to his wife, as if men *ever* paid any attention to vows! The minute their dick sprang to attention, they followed it where ever it led them!

The fear seized me abruptly that his wife might be home.

It flickered through my mind that the woman who had shown me the bathroom might be his wife, but I dismissed that. No one that lived like this tended to their own children. She must be the nanny.

I hoped to *god* she was the nanny!

Why had he brought us here, I wondered?

It was my fault, I realized. I had just sat in his car like a stone and let him figure out what to do with us when I should have been making some kind of suggestion.

I had cried all over him, I realized, feeling humiliated that I had completely lost control.

Kaelen tapped on the door again. "Anna?"

"I'm ok! I'll be out in a few minutes."

I didn't want to go out and face him, but I couldn't very well leave my children unattended by anyone except strangers. It took all I could do to get up. My knees still felt like water. The room spun for a moment when I had finally gained my feet, but I caught myself and moved to the lavatory, splashing cold water in my face until the dizziness finally passed. A short search turned up toothpaste. It was kiddy toothpaste, but I didn't care as long as it would get the horrible taste out of my mouth. When I had brushed my teeth with my finger and gargled, I began to search for some kind of cleanser.

Not surprisingly, there wasn't any, because this was a child's bathroom.

His son's.

I smeared soap on the washcloth I had used to wipe my face and got down on my hands and knees to scrub the area around the toilet. This time Kaelen didn't knock. The door opened. "What the hell are you doing?"

"I'm cleaning up the mess I made," I snapped irritably.

Kaelen crossed the room and crouched beside me. Catching my shoulders, he made he me sit back on my knees. "Leave it. The maids can clean it."

I refused to look him in the eyes. "I'll just rinse it off. I don't want to leave soap on the floor."

He took the soap cloth out of my hand by two fingers and pitched it in the general direction of the lavatory. Catching my face in one hand, he forced my head up. I kept my eyes averted.

The fingers of his other hand stoked along one cheek and then settled on my forehead. "Alexis said you were sick."

I bit my lip, fighting the hysterical giggle that surged in my chest. "She said I barfed."

"Everything's ok now, baby," Kaelen said gently.

I felt my chin wobble. He was wrong. Everything wasn't ok. *Everything* was never going to be completely ok for me again.

I had my girls back, though, I reminded myself. I was going to be all right now.

I looked up at him finally, feeling as if my heart was breaking. I wanted to throw myself at him like his son had and hold on for dear life, but I couldn't do that. "I don't know what I'm going to do now," I managed to say finally. "Is there a hotel around here, you think?"

He gave me a look. "The girls will be fine here for now. Your mother's here, and Marion can help her out."

"My mother's here?" I echoed.

He frowned. "I told you I'd sent her ahead to meet us."

I stared at him blankly. He had meant to bring us here all the time? "We really shouldn't. I can get us a hotel room until I can find a place to stay."

He studied me for a long moment. "You still owe me two weeks."

If he hadn't been holding my jaw it would have hit the floor. I couldn't believe he was crouched here in his *home* with his little boy right outside, demanding that I finish up the two weeks I owed him!

I realized as I stared at him, though, that I was a horrible person, a really horrible person because my heart had leapt when he had said that. I shouldn't even consider going back when I knew now that what I had been doing was wrong.

On the other hand, the only thing that had changed for me was that I was *more* desperate for money than I had been before.

I cleared my throat, tempted to point out to him that he was liable to find himself in the middle of a nasty divorce, but it dawned on me abruptly that he had been with me a solid month. If his wife hadn't shown up screaming bloody murder in all that time, she couldn't care what he was doing, could she? She'd have to have figured out something was up.

I struggled to think if I had ever heard anything about a wife, but the fact was, even though I now knew who he was, I still didn't know anything about him. Would he cheat that openly, I wondered? Or was there no wife for him to worry about? How could there not be when he had a son?

And how was any of that my problem or my business?

I had been hired. I had signed a contract. If he really wanted to push it, he could legally force me to go back. I didn't believe he would. That sort of thing would produce some seriously nasty publicity, and I didn't believe he was like that anyway.

But what did I know?

Rich people didn't get rich from being soft hearted idiots like me.

And everything else aside, he had rescued my children for me. I owed him a hell of a lot more than two weeks! I dismissed my qualms. I had realized going in that I wasn't in a position to quibble over morals, that I couldn't afford to have them. If he was married, he would handle it. "You want me to leave them here for two weeks?" I asked finally.

"They'll be safe. There's plenty of security—both electronic surveillance and round the clock security personnel."

The girls were playing with Kael when we left the bathroom. Alexis ran up to me when she saw me. "His name is Kaelen, too!" she exclaimed, pointing in the general direction of Kaelen's son.

I smiled at her uncomfortably. "That's because Kaelen's his daddy and boys are named for their daddy lots of times."

"Why?"

I stared at her speechlessly. "Because."

"Oh. Can we stay a while?"

I leaned down to hug her. "Yes. Kael ... Mr. Westmoreland invited you to stay, and Grandma, too. Will you be a very good girl if I let you stay?"

She grinned at me. "I'm always a good girl. Ashley's bad."

"You'll have to make sure Ashley behaves, too."

I looked back at them as we reached the door of the playroom. The nanny was trying to round them up and get them off to bed. She had her work cut out for her. I doubted Alexis or Ashley would sleep a wink with a playroom like this just waiting to be fully explored.

I think I was still pretty much in the grips of shock as I got into the car to return to the other mansion with Kaelen. A sense of unreality had swept over me. I was uneasy about my reasoning in my decision to return with Kaelen, but I couldn't dismiss my own needs or concerns, so I dismissed the part I couldn't deal with. I was emotionally exhausted more than anything and fell asleep with my head against the window before we had driven very far. A tug on my hand drew me in the other direction after a while, and I dropped my head onto Kaelen's hard shoulder instead.

I roused when he parked the car, fumbled with my seatbelt, and finally managed to get loose as Kaelen opened the door. He slipped an arm around to lead me inside, and I leaned against him gratefully, allowing him to guide my footsteps.

Gareth was laying in wait when we got inside. Cameron and Dev appeared in the door of the parlor, as well, but Kaelen shook his head at them, walked me upstairs to my room, and helped me to undress. He smiled faintly when he discovered I had nothing on but my jeans and t-shirt. I wasn't sure what he found amusing about it, but I was too tired to take umbrage and merely staggered to the bed and climbed in. I was already half asleep when Kaelen climbed in beside me, dragging me across his chest.

I shouldn't, I thought, and then didn't think of anything else.

****

The sense of walking through a dream didn't really leave me. I suspected it was because I didn't want to let go of it because it comforted me. Oddly enough, the routine of the mansion of ill repute comforted me, too. I hadn't really gotten used to the 'new' routine before my life had fallen apart, but it was familiar enough to give me something to hold on to.

And I relished the time I spent with them. The dream like state that held me actually seemed to make it easier for me to enjoy it ... all of it. Where I had dreaded being alone with any one of them, I opened myself to enjoy it to the fullest. I didn't try not to think about when it would all come to an end, I just didn't.

Kaelen saved the best for last.

I thought so, anyway. In some ways, I was sorry that I couldn't have one last night alone ... with Kaelen, but what we did instead allowed me to be with all of them one last time and that was actually very nice.

Very nice.

I was a little unnerved when Kaelen escorted me upstairs after dinner and I discovered *everyone* was following. More than a little unnerved, actually a little petrified. I thought at first that they had just decided to watch while we did three way, though, and I tried to block out the fact that I had an audience.

I saw, though, as Kaelen helped me out of my dress, that they were undressing, as well.

Still a little perplexed about the proceedings, I waited where Kaelen had left me, watching as he, too, undressed and then moved to the bedside table. He was already erect when he returned with lube and sat on the edge of the bed to smooth it over his cock. He looked up at me when he had finished coating himself thickly. I moved to the bed, but he caught my wrist and told me to move in front of him.

Surprised, I did as he asked, leaning forward as he pulled my hips back against him and then placed his palm on my back. I felt him probe me and concentrated on relaxing the muscles, focused on breathing as he entered me slowly by pulling me back onto his cock until I was sitting on his lap. He shifted the two of us back from the edge, hooking my legs on either side of his and finally leaned back, taking me with him.

I let out a gasp as we moved, as I felt the pressure inside of me increase at the position but warmth filled me as he began to caress my breasts, cupping one in each hand and kneading it. With my eyes half closed with pleasure, I watched as Gareth and Chance approached us. They leaned over me as Kaelen squeezed my breasts in offering. Twin jolts of heat went through me as each of them took a nipple into their mouth and began to tease it. My back already arched by the position Kaelen held me in, I lifted anyway, digging my head against Kaelen's shoulder.

He nuzzled the side of my face and opened his mouth over my ear. His breath and the moist heat of his mouth sent another shot of pleasure through me, and all the while Gareth and Chance tugged at my nipples with their mouths, Kaelen rocked his hips and slowly thrust upward and eased back until I was gasping and moaning with the fire coursing through me from every direction.

"Hold it for me, baby," Kaelen murmured huskily.

I groaned, uncertain if I could, but I struggled to focus my mind away from the pleasure scouring me, held my breath, gasped as the need for air overcame me. Relief flooded me as Gareth and Chance finally ceased to torment me. Chance climbed on the bed, positioned himself above my face and brushed his cock across my lips. I opened my mouth for him, taking him in excitedly, lifting my head to try to take him completely into my mouth as Kaelen continued the rhythm that was slowly driving me insane.

A jolt went through me as I felt the heat of Gareth's mouth on my lower belly and then the flick of a tongue over my clit. I jerked. Kaelen spread his legs wider, spreading mine in the process since my legs were still draped over his.

I groaned as Gareth's mouth began to alternate between tugging at the sensitive bud and sucking it, feeling my body shoot higher, the fire boiling over from my belly to my skin until I felt as if I was burning up. I couldn't be still, and I couldn't move. I sucked on Chance's cock more frantically, until he was groaning as much as I was.

"Just a little more, baby," Kaelen said, his own voice hoarse now, shaking as he fought to hold on to his control.

I was near to coming despite his insistence when the mouth, thankfully, ceased to tease me. A moment later I felt the head of a cock probing the mouth of my sex. Kaelen's arms tightened around me as Gareth thrust, working my juices over his cock until he filled me completely.

I shuddered as he began to move in sync with Kaelen. Chance uttered a choked cry as I tugged and pulled at his cock frantically with my mouth. Groaning, he filled my mouth with his seed.

"Now, baby," Kaelen gasped harshly, "cum for us."

I uttered a low moan, sucking Chance harder as I came.

I was still gasping and moaning and shuddering as Chance pulled his cock from my mouth, fell sideways, and rolled onto his back. Gareth—I had known it was Gareth, leaned over me, hunching his back to suck at first one nipple and then the other. The heat and tension built inside me again as both of them continued to thrust into me, began to move more quickly and then faster still. I clutched at Gareth, groaned as if I was dying as my body took another leap and exploded with ecstasy. Gareth and Kaelen both shuddered as they felt my body quaking around their members. Kaelen ground his teeth, drove deeply inside me, paused for a heartbeat, and then let out a harsh gasp as he pumped his seed into me. Gareth let go of his own control then, pumping into me hard several times before he, too, came.

A shiver skated over me as I lay sandwiched between Gareth and Kaelen, feeling the last throes of their climaxes even as mine mellowed off. After a few moments, Gareth heaved himself upwards and pulled out of me. Swaying on his feet, he caught my hands and pulled me up until I was sitting upright and could slip my legs from Kaelen's. He sat up, lifting me from his lap and settling me again.

I wanted nothing so much as to climb up onto the mattress and collapse, but I made my way to the bathroom and cleaned up. I met Kaelen on my way out. He caught me against him, dipping his head to plant a gusty kiss on my mouth before he let me go.

Cameron and Dev had moved to the bed and Chance and Gareth to the chairs along the wall. I looked at Cameron and Dev tiredly but climbed up on the bed with them.

The last time, I told myself. Tomorrow I was leaving, and I would never see them again.

They had always been considerate. They merely stroked me lazily until I had recovered from the last bout of sex and then we did three way, and then I reversed and gave Cameron head while Dev drove into me.

The mind was willing but the body was weak. I did three way with Chance and Gareth and then, in the aftermath, simply passed out with exhaustion.

I slept late, and I was alone when I woke.

There was nothing different about that, but Kaelen didn't come in as he usually did to wake me and bathe me and help me into that god awful torture devise he loved to see me wear. I took a leisurely bath to try to ease some of the soreness from my muscles and finally dressed, packed my bag, and went downstairs.

I had more than half hoped that I would see them before I left, but there didn't seem to be anyone around. Sighing, trying not to feel badly about it, I left, and got into my car and drove to my mother's house.

My mother and the girls arrived near noon, which had only given me an hour to mope around the house and feel sorry for myself. As thrilled as I was to see my babies again, their incessant chatter about Kaelen and the playroom and Marion, the nanny, set my teeth on edge. I bore with it the best I could, knowing, or at least hoping, that the thrill would wear off in a few days and I wouldn't have to try to smile when they told me about the fun they had had at Kaelen's house.

The third day home I had to fend off their entreaties for me to invite Kael to their house for a visit. I stared at them miserably. "Kael's mommy probably wouldn't like for him to come to stay with us," I said finally.

Alexis stared at me for a moment. "You mean Nanny Marion?"

"No, sweety. Kael's mommy."

Alexis frowned. "She's in heaven, Kael said."

My heart fluttered uncomfortably in my chest. "That's ... so sad for poor little Kael and his daddy," I managed to say finally, feeling terrible that I was relieved to know Kaelen hadn't been cheating on his wife when the poor thing was dead.

I felt even worse that I wanted to pump them for more information. I firmly tamped the urge, not just because it was unseemly to probe about something that personal that wasn't my business, but also because I realized it wasn't good for me to want to know anything about Kaelen.

I was trying hard not to think about any of them. Asking questions of my daughters was just feeding my addiction.

"You can ask his daddy," Ashley volunteered.

The urge to cry swept over me. I swallowed against the knot of emotion with an effort. "I don't work for Kael's daddy anymore."

Alexis frowned. "I thought he was your friend, Mommy?"

I glanced at my mother as she came into the room. "He was ... is," I said hesitantly, trying to feel my way around the landmine. "But he was mostly my boss. He's just a nice person, you know? That's why he took all of us to the zoo, and that's why he invited you and Grandma to stay at his house for a visit."

"Well, why don't you work for him anymore?" Alexis asked.

I couldn't prevent the blush that colored my cheeks. "It was just a short job, sweetheart. And ... uh ... I finished. And now I'm going to go find another job. Why don't we go out in the yard for a little while?" I added, trying to distract them.

They didn't want to go to play in the yard, but I dragged them outside anyway. There was a swing hanging from a tree out back that had been there since I was a little girl. The swing wasn't the same one, of course. That one had long since fallen apart, but it was the same tree, the same limb. They weren't very enthusiastic about it. Kael had a much better swing, a big one that had several swings and a tower and a seesaw.

The list gave me a headache. "Maybe we'll get a nice big swing set kind of like Kael's when we get a place of our own?"

"Daddy's got a nice big house," Ashley offered. "Why don't we go live there?"

"'Cause he's got another wife, stupid," Alexis snapped.

"She called me stupid, Mommy!"

"I heard, Ashley. Don't call your sister stupid, Alexis. That's not nice. We're going to get our own house," I told Ashley firmly,"…without daddy."

There wasn't a chair nearby, so I sat in the grass after a few minutes. I hadn't heard anything from my ex since I had gotten home, but I didn't let them go outside without me or my mother to watch them.

The court day for the hearing had finally been set, and I was looking forward to getting that over with. My lawyer seemed confident that he could get the matter settled quickly and to my advantage. Considering what I was paying him, he had better. I was hoping he could also get the judge to make William cough up child support—which he was supposed to pay regularly and didn't.

I figured if I could somehow get that, and then get a fairly decent paying job, I could quit mooching off my mother and leave her in peace. I wanted to get something in another city, though. William snatching the girls had demolished what little confidence I had had that I could safely live anywhere near him and have a normal life.

Of course my lawyer had informed me that he would get visitation rights, regardless of who was granted custody so, legally, I wouldn't be able to go far, but I was hoping I would be able to work something out where he wouldn't know where I was living and I wouldn't have to watch the girls like a hawk all the time to keep him from grabbing them.

The cop that had come to take the report hadn't helped my feelings with that 'possession being nine tenths' thing. It seemed to me, whatever the court decided, he could still snatch them away if he was of a mind to do it. *Then* it would be kidnapping, but how much good was it going to do me to have the law on my side if he took them and took off somewhere?

Moving seemed like the best idea. Out of sight, I hoped, out of mind. When my ex got tired of trying to get 'even' with me for breathing I could move back so the girls would be able to see their grandmother more regularly.

My lawyer called me a couple of weeks later to inform me that William had withdrawn his petition for custody. I was so stunned I couldn't take it in. Just like that?

The lawyer was going to do something else to make sure that I was named soul guardian of the children so the question wouldn't arise again.

I didn't see that there was anything he could do about that. I had been granted custody in the divorce and William had challenged it, but I didn't know anything about legal things so I didn't argue with him. He had already been paid. He might as well work.

A child support check arrived from William a week after that, which included a healthy percentage of the back support he owed. I nearly fainted when I got that.

I was almost tempted to call William and see if I could find out what was up, but I resisted. I didn't want to talk him, and I doubted I would be able to get a straight answer from him anyway.

As miserable as I was the first few weeks after my 'job' ended, it got worse as time went on, not better. The girls stopped talking about Kael and Kael's house, but I couldn't stop thinking about Kael's daddy, or his uncle, or his cousins.

I found myself scanning the society pages hoping to find some mention of one of them, or maybe a picture. When nothing turned up, I started scanning the legal and financial reports for some mention of one of the many and varied Westmoreland holdings—which I finally realized was the most *seriously* pathetic effort on my part thus far to get any kind of news about them.

It dawned on me after a while that there was really no reason for me to be moping around with my life on hold. The custody situation, as far as I knew, was settled. William had not only paid back support, but another check arrived the very next week. I still had a little money left over from 'the job'. I had planned to go to the local technical school for training, but there were technical schools, I reasoned, in other cities.

I started buying newspapers and studying the help wanted ads and listing of apartments for rent.

I was sitting in the yard with the girls one afternoon with newspapers spread all around me when I heard a car out

front. My heart instantly seized as it leapt into my mind that
it might be William. I stared at the house, listening intently.
The front door opened, but I didn't hear my mother
screeching so I relaxed and went back to circling job
possibilities.

I didn't even look up when the back door opened and
closed again. "Who was it, Mom?"

Instead of answering, I heard footsteps coming across the
yard. Twisting around to see who it was, I felt my heart just
stop in my chest.

"Kaelen!" Alexis whooped, diving out of the swing and
racing across the yard with Ashley at her heels trying to
keep up.

I couldn't get up. I couldn't even breathe. Kaelen stopped
when the girls collided with him, smiling down at them
good naturedly while they bounced around him like frisky
puppies demanding to know if he had brought Kael with
him.

My mother, who I finally saw had followed him out the
back door, began to scold the girls and told them to go
inside. I couldn't find my voice or I would have vetoed
that. I didn't want to be left alone with Kaelen! I needed
them to distract me. I needed a buffer.

They pouted, but they went inside, and Kaelen crossed the
yard to where I was sitting. Stopping in front of me, he
shoved his hands into his pant's pockets. I stared up at him,
unable to think of anything to say. Finally, he crouched
down. "How've you been, Anna?"

I swallowed with an effort. "Fine," I managed. "You?"

He sat down, scrubbing a hand over his face. He looked
tired. It made me ache to see it. I couldn't help but worry
that something was wrong. "Actually, not worth a shit."

I blinked in surprise. I had been expecting the usual 'fine'
and I didn't know what to say. "I'm sorry," I said finally.
"There's not … a problem, is there? I mean, Kael's
alright?"

He sucked in a harsh breath. "He's fine … couldn't stop
talking about Alexis and Ashley. He misses them."

I smiled faintly. "They miss him, too. They wanted me to
ask you to let him come stay with them awhile, but I
explained to them that he couldn't." I shrugged. "They
don't really understand."

He frowned. "Understand what?"

There was something about his expression that urged me to proceed with care. "That you just took them in for me … to help us out and …. Well, I'd love to have him come to visit, but we don't really have room … not here," I finished lamely. "How's Gareth?" I added quickly, changing the subject.

His frown deepened. "Miserable. And before you ask, Cameron, and Dev, and Chance, too … not to mention me."

My heart fluttered in my chest. "I'm … sorry to hear that. They're alright, though?"

"Except for being miserable as hell, you mean?"

I looked at him in distress. "Something's wrong?"

"Every damn thing is wrong, baby!" Kaelen growled.

I lay the paper in my lap aside and moved closer, placing a hand on his knee. "You're scaring me, Kael. Everything can't be all right if they're miserable and you're miserable! Tell me!"

He gave me a look I found hard to interpret. "And you'll make it better?"

I blushed. He hadn't said it sarcastically, though. "If I can. *Is* there something I can do?"

He wrapped his hand around my wrist, giving me a hard yank that brought me flying forward. I slammed into him, bowling him over and sprawling on his chest. Wrapping his arms around me, he rolled until I was underneath him looking up. His smile was unnerving. "As a matter of fact, there is *something* you can do," he murmured, then lifted his head and surveyed the yard. "You think your mother will keep the girls in the house?"

I reddened. "Kaelen!"

He rolled off of me, but he didn't get up. Instead, he propped his head in his hand and reached into his jacket with his other hand. Bringing out a folded sheaf of papers, he handed it to me. I stared at it for several moments, looked at him questioningly and finally opened it up. After scanning the legalese for several moments and arriving at no better understanding than if it had been written in a foreign language, I looked at him again. "I don't really understand legal documents that well," I said apologetically.

I watched his Adam's apple bob as he swallowed. "It's pre-nup."

I frowned in puzzlement and looked at the papers again. "For who?"

He reddened. "You."

Stunned, I blinked at him. "Why would I need a pre-nup?"

His face went taut. "*I* need the pre-nup. I can't get married without it."

I couldn't help it, my chin wobbled. "You're getting married?"

Kaelen stared at me for a long moment and finally reached to hook a hand behind my head. Dragging me down, he opened his mouth over mine and kissed me until I was drunk from the heated sensations flowing through me. "*We* are getting married," he said when he broke the kiss at last.

I stared up at him, feeling as if my eyes were rolling around independently of each other, but it hit me then, finally, that he was asking me to marry him. I promptly burst into tears. It was the worst proposal I had ever … not heard!

He studied me uneasily. "Is that a no?"

I uttered a watery chuckle. "Kaelen! You are so … you didn't even *ask* me! I couldn't figure out what you were talking about!"

He frowned, apparently thinking it over. An expression of discomfort crossed his features. "Is that a no, then?"

Mastering the tears, I dragged in a sustaining breath and let it out slowly. I wasn't going to get anything else out of him, but what more did I need? "Of course!" I said, dragging him down for another kiss.

"Of course, what?" he asked, peeling me off.

I looked at him blankly for a moment before I realized what I had said. I shook my head. "I love you. Did you bring a pen?"

"You didn't read it."

"Because I can't understand one word out of ten, and it doesn't matter … not to me. You're sure you want to marry me?" I added worriedly.

He grinned at me and kissed me until my eyes rolled back in my head. "I *know* what I want," he murmured huskily when he lifted his head at last.

I frowned at him. "Don't I at least get an 'I love you, too?"

He chuckled. "You didn't seem to want to get an 'I love you' from me out here in your mother's backyard, but if you insist...."

He *did* love me ... for hours and hours on our honeymoon—which we spent entirely by ourselves. When we got back, we honeymooned with Gareth and Cameron and quite often Chance and Dev, as well, because I had a seriously kinky husband and I happened to enjoy being with his equally kinky brother and cousins because I adored them almost as much as I adored Kaelen.

I finally got around to asking Kaelen on our first anniversary why it was that they chose me instead of each of them picking a woman for themselves.

Kaelen studied me doubtfully for several moments and finally shrugged. "We tried that the first time around, but they didn't 'do' submissive worth a damn. All of us wanted to swap—not because any of the women were that great but because none of us were happy with the ones we had picked—and they fought."

It wasn't exactly the answer I had expected, but I couldn't help but smile. "They fought?"

He grunted.

"Soooo ... you decided just to pick one?"

His eyes gleamed, but he shook his head, leaning down to kiss me. "We decided just to pick you."

I smiled at him. "You're just saying that because you don't want me to be mad."

He chuckled. "I don't, but it's the truth. We *all* picked you. After arguing about it a while, when I saw nobody was going to pick anyone else, we decided just to go with the one we wanted—you."

I grinned at him. "You are *so* good, I almost believe you."

He laughed. "Ask them."

I did. They told me the same thing.

I *knew* they were smart!

The End

Printed in the United States
120658LV00001B/61-108/A

9 781586 088996